Cartucho and *My Mother's Hands*

The Texas Pan American Series

Cartucho

and

My Mother's Hands

By Nellie Campobello

Translated by Doris Meyer and Irene Matthews
Introduction by Elena Poniatowska

UNIVERSITY OF TEXAS PRESS
AUSTIN

Translation of *Cartucho,* © 1931, and *Las manos de Mamá,* © 1938, by Nellie Campobello
Introduction copyright © 1988 by Elena Poniatowska
Translations copyright © 1988 by the University of Texas Press
Printed in the United States of America
First edition, 1988
Requests for permission to reproduce material from this work should be sent to:
  Permissions
  University of Texas Press
  Box 7819
  Austin, Texas 78713-7819

Library of Congress Cataloging-in-Publication Data

Campobello, Nellie.
  Cartucho ; and, My mother's hands.

  (The Texas Pan American series)
  Translation of: Cartucho and Las manos de mamá.
  1. Mexico—History—Revolution, 1910—Fiction.
I. Campobello, Nellie. Manos de mamá. English. 1988.
II. Title.   III. Title: Cartucho.   IV. Title: My mother's
hands.   V. Series.
PQ7297.C2448C3713   1988   863   87-25462

ISBN 978-0-292-71111-2

The Texas Pan American Series is published with the assistance of a revolving publication
fund established by the Pan American Sulphur Company.

Contents

That woman with regal carriage sweeping the air with her arms is called Nellie Campobello. That woman with her hair pulled back stretching her neck and pointing one toe is Nellie. Gloria and Nellie are dancing in their School of Dance. They twirl around, their skirts like corollas. From above they look like huge flowers: Mexican dahlias formed of a dozen petticoats.

"Now, a dance from Jalisco."

The two sisters give a demonstration.

"You must make your body speak, give it more meaning."

Nellie launches herself. This is her moment, her body movements are immediately noticeable. They are a faster form of expression than writing. And they have an immediate response, too. Clustered against the walls, her pupils watch her admiringly.

"Mexicans are silent, canny, I mean the people who live in the country. The way they move is the way they really express themselves."

The two sisters are now teaching Mayan rhythms.

"Stronger, shorter steps. The mestizo's way of walking is both graceful and concise."

Nellie laughs.

"Well, the Mayans are not as tall as I am; so there's almost a biological reason why their dance tempos and steps are short, light, and lively."

Nellie and Gloria Campobello have traveled from one end of Mexico to the other, collecting indigenous rhythms. The Indians they love the most are the Tarahumarans, for the sisters are a part of their land. The two northerners go to all the fiestas, and if there isn't one on, they sit in the central plazas and watch what's happening. From their notes, from the loving gaze they cast upon Mexico, are born words in motion: "The native of Mexico State," they write, "walks with his body weight over his heels, like the people from the Yucatán except that unlike them, he doesn't stretch his body up nor tilt it backward, rather he leans forward, although not so much as the Michoacán Indian . . . With his eyes always fixed on the ground and with his arms tucked tight against his body, he gives the impression that as he walks he is embracing himself."

In 1940, Nellie is known as a ballerina, choreographer, ballet teacher. She is especially interested in prehispanic dance. "Indigenous dance is the purest expression of Mexico." Named Director of the National School of

Dance in 1937, Nellie is one of its founders; from there she immerses herself in our culture and brings it to life. Mexico unveils itself. Nellie unveils her creative capacity, the strength of her great country.

Its poverty, mistrust, betrayal, and violence . . . she lived them all in her childhood in Villa Ocampo and Parral, Durango; but she could still declare, "I was quite a happy child," for in her childhood her mother knew how to create another world: a charmed world that mitigated the immediate reality—the harshness of Revolution.

In the parish church of Villa Ocampo—where, above all, the people have fond memories of their native daughter and benefactress (the local school bears her name)—lie the records of the birth of María Francisca, born on the 7th of April 1900, natural daughter of Rafaela Luna. Nellie invented more recent birthdates, 1907, 1909. And Doña Concha Encarnación Estrada, at ninety years old, remembers playing with Nellie as a little girl, then called "Xica" (for Francisca) and a couple of years younger than Concha.

In an interview with Carlos Landeros in number 301 of the cultural supplement of *Siempre!* in 1957, Martín Luis Guzmán declared: "Probably nothing has given me more satisfaction, apart from my personal acquaintance with Villa, than having in my own hands Villa's personal archive that is kept by his widow, Doña Austreberta Rentería, and that Señorita Nellie Campobello brought to me when she interviewed me—some thirty years ago—as a part of a full portrait of Francisco Villa proposed to help the Villa cause . . . Thanks to those papers I got the idea for the right form for the *Memorias de Pancho Villa* (*Memoirs of Pancho Villa*) and in fact the first three hundred pages of the *Memorias* are based to a great extent on those same papers." Later on he emphasizes: "One day, I believe, we will all know about that personality I mentioned a moment ago, that admirable young lady, Nellie Campobello, who has been a staunch admirer, a tireless defender, of the person and the memory of Pancho Villa for more than forty years . . ."

Don Martín finished the five books of the *Memorias de Pancho Villa* with the battles in the Bajío, before the downfall of the warrior. Nellie Campobello, despite her unquenchable enthusiasm, finishes her *Apuntes sobre la vida militar de Pancho Villa* with the compromising truce of the chief and his withdrawal to the Canutillo hacienda given to him by the revolutionary government.

Martín Luis Guzmán shows through the character of Axkaná González in *La sombra del caudillo* that ineptitude and corruption converted into governing power have existed for over fifty years and that there is no doubt about "the tragedy of the politician caught in the web of immorality and lies that he himself has spun"; the aging Mariano Azuela rails against the profiteers, the big landowners, the local chieftains, the new rich, the venal leaders who betrayed the ideals of the Revolution; but to Nellie Campobello it seems that the Revolution has revindicated the rights and the dignity of the people and that the heroes who emerged from the people are our lay saints. A true devotee, she most strongly defends Pancho Villa, her hero, her idol—despite the bloody orgies—her Golden Soldier to whom she dedicates hours and days of research, with his troops and fighters: Nieto, Dávila, and Maynez, Nellie collects testimonies—from one of his widows, Austreberta Rentería—and writes it all down, passionately. In spite of her admiration, of all her books *Apuntes sobre la vida militar de Francisco Villa* is the least significant. Uncritical, Nellie chooses to see only the wood, never the trees. Jesusa Palancares, the protagonist of *Hasta no verte Jesús mío,* has a much more critical view of the Mexican Revolution, although she could neither read nor write. She says: "I think it was a bad war because that business of killing each other off, fathers against sons, brothers against brothers; Carranza's men, and Villa's, and Zapata's . . . well that was a lot of nonsense 'cos we were all in the same boat: poor as church mice and half dead of starvation. But those are the things that, as they say, everyone knows and nobody ever tells." Jesusa doesn't have the same image of Francisco Villa left to us by Nellie, either: "Villa was a bandit because he didn't fight like a man but boasted of dynamiting the tracks as the trains went by. . . . If there's anyone I really hate, it's Villa."

Almost fifty years have gone by and, as Adolfo Gilly says: "The Mexican bourgeoisie's affirmation that the 'revolution lives' is the negative confirmation of the permanent nature of the interrupted revolution." Octavio Paz is even more condemnatory: "Every revolution that has no critical thought, no freedom to contradict the powerful and no possibility of peaceful substitution of one government for another, is a revolution that is self-defeating."

With her strong, singular personality, so important in dance and the Mexican dance movement, member of the group of writers of the Revolution, Nellie never received the recognition that would stimulate her vocation as a writer. If she had, she would not now be eighty-seven years old and isolated in Tlaxcala, far from the community of writers. The mere fact that key characters in the culture of our country, like Orozco, Martín Luis Guzmán and Carlos Pellicer, endorse them gives the Campobello sisters (whose biography still waits in the wings) the value that has been so stingily accorded elsewhere. The cruelty that cradled Nellie's childhood enfolds her old age, too.

The Mexican Revolution is institutionalized and also novelized. Six years after it begins, in 1916, Mariano Azuela publishes *Los de abajo* (*The Underdogs*), the novel of the Mexican Revolution par excellence, which opens the floodgates with the character Demetrio Macías, of whom Azuela himself admitted: "If I had known a man of his stature, I would have followed him to the death." From Azuela on, the novel of the Revolution takes off at a gallop: Martín Luis Guzmán produces *La sombra del caudillo* and *El águila y la serpiente* (*The Eagle and the Serpent*), giving Mexico the best prose it had known to date. Guzmán is followed by Gregorio López y Fuentes, Rafael F. Muñoz, José Ruben Romero, José Vasconcelos, Francisco L. Urquizo, José Mancisidor, Mauricio Magdaleno, Agustín Yáñez, and José Revueltas. Among them one single woman: Nellie Campobello. The publication in 1958 of *La región más transparente* (*Where the Air Is Clear*), by Carlos Fuentes, gives the novel of the Revolution its second wind, since Rulfo and his *Pedro Páramo* (1955) are a different phenomenon. Fuentes' important work opens the door to Arturo Azuela (nephew of the first Azuela), to Fernando del Paso, to Ibargüengoitia, for whom the Revolution is a huge joke, to Tomás Mojarro, and once again to a single woman: Elena Garro, who to a certain extent is Nellie Campobello's successor. Ibargüengoitia's *Los relámpagos de agosto* (*The Lightning of August*) flips the other side of the coin—a comic, uninhibited Revolution, a Revolution to be made fun of, a Revolution that doesn't take itself seriously, that flees from tragedy, while Rulfo is the very essence of the tragic. *It may be that Nellie Campobello's is the only real vision of the Mexican Revolution written by a woman.* When she dedicates her *Apuntes sobre la vida militar de Francisco Villa* to Guzmán, naming him the best revolutionary writer of the Revolution, she doesn't recognize that she is the best woman writer of the Revolution. Her words—freed from adjectives and embellishments— her direct, almost raw, style, belong to an Adelita who is off to join the battle.

Nellie Campobello publishes *Cartucho: Relatos de la lucha en el norte* in Ediciones Integrales in 1931, yet of all the novelists of the Revolution she is the one who gets the least notice. In a *macho* world, she is not taken into account, and—give me a break—what's a woman doing at the shotgun orgy, anyway? That's all we need; Nellie's too amusing, Nellie's too descriptive, Nellie's too "clever," so she is relegated to giving impressions, brilliant images seen from the balcony: a curious creature leafing inadvertently through a ghastly book that has nothing to do with her. And that's how she tells it, naïvely, with the candor of childhood: scenes that astonish in their cruelty and because they are witnessed by a little girl.

Death by Bullets: Her Familiar World

From having seen so many bloody deeds, Nellie thought that she could tell the future; after all, she was well acquainted with death, since everyone fell right outside her window, like stringless puppets. The sharp, wise little girl is also a temperamental little girl, tempted by danger, a little girl who is not and never will be a little girl, except at her mother's hands; or perhaps a little girl who never grew up and petrified inside that slim body, made for dancing (the Campobello sisters were very beautiful). Nellie doesn't invent anything she tells; she saw, she lived, she recorded it all. Her vision was not that gentle contemplation of other normal little girls, but episodes of brutality, of monstrous atrocity. The only sweetness in her life comes from those two hands, her mother's hands, and at the age when other children's heads lie on the pillow and listen to their mothers sing of "Little golden sparrows . . . in a crystal cage," Nellie doesn't recall snowy swans and fairy princes: her only swans are Villa and his Golden Boys, the only real characters are the Villa men who take her in their arms, give her her favorite chewy caramels. For Nellie, there are no little old grandmamas, only wolves, and as Antonio Castro Leal says, the intrepid Nellie "never gets frightened, nor sentimental." The one thing that moves her is the memory of her mother, a peaceful haven in the thick of the bullets. Nellie marries off her dolls to nice young revolutionaries. And if fate doesn't smile on the chosen one, the engagement is easily undone! "No, no; he was never Pitaflora's boyfriend . . ." She—daughter of a father lost on the battlefield of Ojinaga—picks out a corpse for herself; right outside her house. She thinks rather pretty General Sobarzo's rosy innards. She watches firing squads, sees men hanged, witnesses the most summary of judgments, all with the delicious freshness of someone watching a great show with neither nostalgia for the past nor plans for the future: "a virgin vision of the Revolution."

The Childhood of Revolution or the Child of the Revolution

Ever since, Nellie writes as if she were firing bullets. Her sentences always hit the bull's eye, scorch with their directness, their absolute lack of elaboration. Unlike other writers of the Revolution, Nellie never criticizes it; on the contrary, she maintains almost as much devotion for the Revolution as she does for her mother. She feels no mistrust; everything it does is well done, everything can be justified, everything has its reason. She is still the little girl who sees a group of ten men take aim at one young man on his knees, badly wounded, his hands outstretched toward the soldiers, already dying from fear. She notices with interest how the body gives a terrible leap as the bullets hit it, how the blood gushes from numerous holes. It lies three days next to her window and Nellie gets used to the scrawny pile; when someone or other carries it off in the night, she misses it. "That dead body really belonged to me."

Accustomed to violence, to cruelty, Nellie's familiar world is the world of executed men. They are a part of her childhood. In *Las manos de Mamá* she bequeathes us memorable pages about her mother, the real one and the other one: the Revolution. Her mother is a heroine who, as well as sewing on her machine to support her children, runs out to save people dear to her, and runs back in again to hem petticoats, turn up cuffs for little girls of school age. But "What was the poor little noise of that machine compared with the shouts of the cannon? . . . How many pounds of flesh would they come to in total? How many eyes and thoughts?" Strange little girl who thinks of heavy gunfire as a song and talks of the pounds of flesh made up by the dead bodies.

Rulfo as a child saw the sinister puppets of the hanged men, and no one covered Nellie's eyes, either; on the contrary, they were opened wide to see all the better. In *Mis libros* she says: "More than three hundred men shot in as many moments, inside a barracks, leaves a big, big impression—so people said—but our childish eyes found it quite normal."

Nellie uses some very happy turns of phrase: "Jiménez is a dusty little town. Its streets are like hungry tripes." The little girl who drinks coffee with sugared bread, milk with sweet potato (curiously enough, Jesusa Palancares also likes milk with sweet potato best) accepts her fate presided over by a wonderful mother. "My life was a counterpane of colors." Nellie writes fast, doesn't pay much attention to style. "You have to do things quickly. That way you don't feel frightened."

What does a writer do when her childhood is a battlefield? What does a little girl do when her friends are men on horseback galloping into her house and scarring the hallway with their hooves? What does a girl do when she is born in Mexico with the new century and she's going to see not only the landscape after the fighting but also the birth of the Mexico that emerges from the roots of the Revolution and where everything has to be done, everything has to be invented, education and health, art and play, language and freedom and loving love between equal partners? For the Campobello sisters dancing the Revolution are a part of that effervescence that spills over in the twenties and whose fascination still hasn't died down. Mexico is transformed through the toil and the magic of its art into a lodestone; lured by our so-called Renaissance come André Breton and Antonin Artaud, Emily Edwards, Edward Weston, Tina Modotti, D. H. Lawrence, Anita Brenner, Frances Toor, Carleton Beals, William Spratling, and, later, Anna Seghers, Valle Inclán, Graham Greene, and many many more. The walls of Mexico are potential frescoes; they exist to be painted on. History will spread itself before the eyes of the people in huge images that will teach them their true worth; Diego Rivera is painting, and Siqueiros; and Orozco, in love with Gloria Campobello, illustrates *Las manos de Mamá* by her sister Nellie: not only muralism is important, it's also a time for ways of living, ways of loving, to flourish in Mexico. Miguel and Rosa Covarrubias set out to cover the entire republic unearthing prehispanic relics, and after their book on Bali they publish their extraordinary *Mexico South*. Lupe Marín is a black panther and one day when Diego Rivera doesn't give her any money for the market, she serves him up for lunch a delicious stew of pottery shards. Dr. Atl, Julio Castellanos, Roberto Montenegro, Fito Best Maugard, the Contemporáneos, Rufino Tamayo, Rodríguez Lozano, Juan O'Gorman—the twenties and thirties are extraordinarily fertile for Mexico. Lázaro Cárdenas opens the doors to Spanish refugees, as earlier they were opened to Trotsky. The muralists attract many foreigners; mural painting is a center of energy, mural painting displaces the art from one continent with another newly emergent. Admiration is now directed to Mexico as it was to Florence; to Teotihuacan as it was to Cheops; to Chichen Itzá and Uxmal as it was to the Coliseum, to the new nation that erupted from its own battles and that conquered, alone and before the Russian Revolution, its liberty.

Contemporary of Extraordinary Women

Nellie Campobello is the contemporary of a series of extraordinary women: María Izquierdo, Frida Kahlo, Leonora Carrington, Remedios Varo, Lupe Marín, Nahui Olín, María Asúnsolo, Dolores del Río. She belongs to a Mexico in the process of discovering itself and fascinated by itself and fascinating other seers, this Mexico-divine-Narcissus, this Mexico-creole-Ulysses, this Mexico-Prometheus-enchained, Mexico naming itself and appearing on the face of the earth, Mexico of the creation and of the seventh day, that without ado sets out to name the things of the earth, to turn them over to see how and of what they are made, to spread them out in the evening like Carlos Pellicer who with his Brother Sun places the evenings any old where, sky up and earth down like the great Olmec heads scattered like meteorites in Tabasco's jungles. The Mexican Revolution is an authentic popular movement; some women also stand tall and toss their angry heads long before any feminist movement in Latin America. Splendid figures like Concha Michel, Benita Galeana, and Magdalena Mondragón, although their works are not the equal of their heroic profiles. A northerner like Nellie, Magdalena Mondragón is the nonconformist author of *Los presidentes me dan risa*, banned in the bookstores as subversive.

Being a trooper means tightening one's belt, having a staunch heart and a strong character. These two women writers know what they are up against, and if not, they intuit it. Nevertheless, Nellie is not an activist, she has no political ambition whatsoever (the Revolution cured her once and for all); nor does she want any type of honors (although she regrets that she is not recognized as she should be in literature). She sticks to her art: dance and literature, literature and dance; the *danse macabre* of the Revolution alongside the dance that should be created in our country, the dance that integrates its multiple, different aspects, popular dance whose clacking heels should be a part of the formal dance schools and solidify the country's nationalism with the steps that come from far off and tell of the people, the *adelitas,* the rhymes and sayings, the *ayayays* that fly across the guitar strings. As Concha Michel gathers in one book the entire republic in its *corridos,* verses, and popular rhythms, Nellie and her sister "Gloriecita," as she calls her, collect steps and movements, arms and legs, her mother's steps on the earth, her mother the essential figure in her life, her guide through life, " . . . she gave us her songs; her feet embroidered dance steps for us" . . . Orozquian figures, Guzmanian figures, revolutionary figures, suffering figures, newborn figures, birthing figures. "Mama, dance for me, sing, give me your voice. . . . I want to see you embroider your eternal dance for me."

"Mama, turn your head. Smile as you did then, twirling in the wind like a red poppy that is shedding its petals."

And this plea from the depths: ". . . and I, a woman now, dressed in white and without makeup, cried out over the door: 'Mama, Mama, Mama!'"

(*Translated by Irene Matthews*)

· *Cartucho* ·

Tales of the Struggle in Northern Mexico

..

By Nellie Campobello
Translated by Doris Meyer

The elderly wisp of a woman I met in 1983, in a dilapidated house a few blocks from the Paseo de la Reforma, seemed to have lost contact with the boisterous Mexican reality at her doorstep. She inhabited a world of memories and visions with only a passing interest in discussing her works, which had struck me so powerfully when I read them some months before. I later learned that Nellie Campobello was considered an eccentric long before she reached old age.

Even at the peak of her career, Nellie Campobello lived, as Emmanuel Carballo put it, "in a different and distant dimension compared to most Mexican writers . . . In her person, just as in her home, the past and present, literature and dance, coexist." Unconventional, unmarried by choice, and a professional dancer as well as a writer, Campobello was a free spirit in a society that expected women to conform to traditional Hispano-Catholic values. She spent most of her adult life in Mexico City, yet she remained fiercely loyal to the northern region around Durango where she grew up in the turmoil and violence of the Mexican Revolution. Despite her privileged background and education, she was outspoken in her defense of Francisco (Pancho) Villa, the peasant hero of the North. The paradoxes of her unusual life—including being the only female among the principal writers of the revolution—may explain in part why Campobello was never accorded the recognition she deserves.

Cartucho, first published in 1931, is a vivid evocation of war seen through a young girl's eyes. Often called a novel, it is in fact a blend of autobiography, history, and poetry. In fifty-six rapid sketches that have the quality of cinematic vision—"children's lives, if no one emprisons them, are an uncut film," wrote Campobello—*Cartucho* is both a tribute to the common soldier and a denunciation of war. The language of the child narrator is direct, unadorned, and authentically Mexican. But Campobello has said elsewhere that what seems so naïve was in fact a deliberate technique or "discipline." Choosing a child's voice and viewpoint, born of her own experience and knowledge, allowed her "to use its apparent unconsciousness to convey what I knew had to be said sincerely and directly." The result is so convincing that many readers have overlooked the artistry that lies behind it.

It was during a visit to Cuba, at the bedside of a hospitalized friend who wanted to hear Nellie's remembrances of the revolution, that the idea came to her to write *Cartucho.* Each afternoon she would bring him the jottings she had made in a green notebook the night before, "stories that seemed invented but weren't." When *Cartucho* was eventually published, the author found herself passionately denounced by anti-Villa partisans; the post-revolutionary Mexican bourgeoisie wanted no rekindling of *villista* populism. One wonders if the changes Campobello made for a second edition in 1940 were at least partially in response to those criticisms; in that edition, she deleted some of the autobiographical and historical references and expanded the multivocal aspects of the narrative to create a work with strong epic resonances. *Cartucho* is the testimony of a child, but it is also the testimony of many common people of the North told to Nellie or to her mother—a woman of heroic proportions, comparable to Villa in another domain. The counterpoint of these voices, narrated by the child witness, is a literary rendering of the spirit of the Mexican *corrido,* the anonymous folk ballads so popular during the revolution.

I have chosen to retain the original Spanish title for my translation of *Cartucho* because the English equivalent, "cartridge," has none of the Spanish rhythm and feeling. When I asked Campobello why she chose this title and what she meant by the first sketch portraying a soldier by that name, she spoke of the unpredictability of life in towns like her own, Hidalgo del Parral, where people lived precariously close to death and dealt with highly charged emotions that might explode at any moment. For her, the vagaries of war were a lot like those of love, and thus Cartucho was "done in" as much by his sentimentality as by his bravado.

For this translation, I have used the second edition, considered definitive by the author, reprinted in a personal collection of her works entitled *Mis libros (My Books)* (Mexico City: Compañía General de Ediciones, 1960), which also contains a lengthy autobiographical prologue on which I have drawn for this note. I should like to add that I have tried to reproduce as faithfully as possible the idiosyncratic syntax and phraseology of Campobello's Spanish, incorporating occasional *mexicanismos* into the translation.

This book is the combined effort of two translators dealing with works that are closely related in time and setting but different in style. *Cartucho* and *My Mother's Hands* are natural companion pieces, but the author's voice in the latter is more intensely lyrical, reflecting the intimacy of her subject. Irene Matthews and I had each met Campobello and decided to translate her work prior to meeting each other and collaborating on this publication. We have worked separately, I in Connecticut and she in California, but with a shared desire to bring Campobello's writing to the attention of a wider public.

D.M.

..

*To Mama, who gave me the gift of true stories
in a country where legends are invented and
where people lull their pain listening to them.*

..

I
MEN OF THE NORTH

Cartucho didn't say his name. He didn't know how to sew or replace buttons. One day his shirts were brought to our house. Cartucho came to say thank you. "Money sometimes makes people forget how to laugh," I said, playing under a table. Cartucho took off the big sombrero he was wearing and, with his eyes half closed, said, "Goodbye." How nice he was! A real *cartucho!*

One day he sang something about love. His voice sounded very pretty. Tears ran down his cheeks. He said he was a *cartucho* because of a woman. He used to play with my little sister Gloria and give her horseback rides. Up and down the street.

A time came when they said the Carranzistas were going to arrive. The Villistas went out to buy cigarettes, holding on to their 30-30s. Cartucho came to visit. He would sit in the window and stare at the crack in a lavender flagstone. Or he'd wipe Gloria's runny nose and improvise little slippers for her with his handkerchiefs. One afternoon he took her in his arms and walked up the street. Suddenly, shots rang out. Cartucho, with little Gloria in his arms, was firing in the direction of La Cruz Hill from the corner where Don Manuel lived. He had already fired several volleys when they took her away from him. After that the shooting got heavy. Houses were closed up. No one knew what happened to Cartucho. He had kept on firing his rifle from the corner.

A few days went by. He didn't appear. Mama asked about him. Then José Ruiz, from over in Balleza, told her, "Cartucho has finally found what he was looking for."

José Ruiz said, "There is only one song, and that was the one Cartucho was singing."

José was a philosopher. His blond hair, parted in the middle and greased down with suet, hung limp from the cold. The keen eyes of a yellow dog. He spoke synthetically and thought with the Bible on the tip of his rifle.

"Love made a *cartucho* of him. And us? . . . *Cartuchos.*" So he said, in a philosophic prayer, buckling on his cartridge belt.

Tall, cinnamon skin, chestnut hair, green eyes, two gold eyeteeth—they had been knocked out in a fight when he was laughing. He hollered a lot when he rode his horse. He always got drunk on sotol. "Viva Elías Acosta!" people shouted when he passed through our neighborhood of Segunda del Rayo.* Elías was the model of a handsome man. He wore jaguar-skin chaps, a new pistol, and a general or colonel's leather jacket. When he wanted to have fun, he practiced target shooting at the hats of men who walked by on the street. He never killed anybody. He was just playing, and no one got angry with him.

Elías Acosta was famous for being a Villista, for being brave, and for being good. He was born in the town of Guerrero, in the state of Chihuahua. He knew how to cry at the memory of his mother. He'd laugh when he fought and when they called him "Shewolf." He was quite elegant, and I think thousands of girls were in love with him. One day, riding by our house, very drunk, he got off his horse, sat down on the ledge of the window, and drew lots of pictures of monkeys for us. Then he wrote down all of our names and said he'd be our friend. He gave each of us a bullet from his pistol. The color of his face was very pretty: it looked like a ripe peach. His assistant helped him mount his horse. Off he went singing. That day he had hit his target.

---

*Also called "the second street of El Rayo" or "Segunda del Rayo Street," this was where Nellie lived as a child in Hidalgo del Parral, an important town on the main rail line between Durango and Chihuahua, with her mother, Rafaela Luna, and her brothers and sisters. Her father, a Villista general killed in battle in 1914, was an unfeeling parent in her memory, so Nellie adopted the Hispanicized form of the name of her stepfather, Stephen Campbell, when her mother remarried some years later. (Trans.)

Kirilí wore a red jacket and yellow leather chaps. He liked to show off his singing because people would say, "Kirilí, what a fine voice you have!" On his little finger he wore a wide ring that he'd taken off a dead man back in Durango. He courted Chagua, a lady with tiny feet. Whenever fighting broke out, Kirilí would pass through Segunda del Rayo often so folks could see him firing shots. He walked with a swagger and an easy smile, like a buttonhole, on his face.

Whenever he set to talking about combat, he'd say that he had killed nobody but generals, colonels, and majors. He never killed foot soldiers. Sometimes Gándara and El Peet told him not to be such a liar. Doña Magdalena, his mother, loved him a lot and admired him.

Off they went to Nieves. Kirilí was taking a bath in a river when someone told him the enemy was coming, but he didn't believe it and didn't get out of the water. They arrived and killed him right there, in the river.

Chagua dressed in mourning, and not long after that she became a streetwalker.

Doña Magdalena, who no longer has any teeth and wears eyeglasses for reading, cries for him every day in a corner of her house in Chihuahua. But El Kirilí lay there in the water, his body turning cold, the tissue of his porous flesh clutching the bullets that killed him.

Bustillos had been born in San Pablo de Balleza. Whenever he came to Parral he brought two or three friends with him, and they'd come to the house to see Mama. They talked about the revolution. Colonel Bustillos loved to see how angry Mama would get when they said anything at all about Villa. He didn't hate the Jefe, he told her, but he never liked to hear people praise him. He thought that Villa was just like anyone else and that when the day came for him to die, he would die just like the others. Bustillos had a handlebar mustache that was wider than his face, and he always twirled the right tip with his fingers. He walked slowly, had light skin and blue eyes. His face looked like a scared rabbit's. He never laughed, and he knew how to speak Mayo.* Never in military uniform, he wore a white Stetson hat and navy blue suit, a tight cartridge belt and a pistol at his left side. He'd stay in town three or four days and spend almost all that time in our house. Our pet doves delighted him. One that was a slate gray color used to beat up the others; he was such a bully that he terrified them all. Colonel Bustillos was very amused by him. One day he said to Mama, "This bird is a real Pancho Villa." Mama didn't say anything, but when Bustillos left, she would caress her Pancho Villa every day.

The dove, after his reputation as Pancho Villa got around, was found dead one day with his head shot off. Mama got very angry. We roasted it over a cow dung fire in the corral. Colonel Bustillos helped us pluck the feathers. I think he shot the bird himself.

Mama said that once in Parral, in the Francos' house during a break in the fighting, the General himself asked her, "I wonder who killed your Pancho Villa?"

---

*The Mayo Indians are a tribe indigenous to the state of Sonora in northwest Mexico. (Trans.)

Bartolo came from Santiago Papasquiaro, Durango. He had a narrow mouth, eyes with no sparkle, and wide hands. He killed the man his sister ran off with, and he was dodging the law. That's why he became a soldier. Bartolo used to sing "Banished was I." He said that if his sister ran off it was because she was a rolling stone. "I killed the first one so she'd have to look for another. She'll keep on rolling, and she meant more to me than anything in my life."

He took up with Anita. She accepted him out of fear. "Banished was he by the government," he would sing through closed lips, and when tears came to his eyes, he slid his sombrero forward. He didn't want to find his sister, because she meant more to him than anything in his life. He used to sit on a high balustrade across from Anita's house with his legs dangling over the side. I admired him because he was so high up, and when he swung his legs it looked like he was going to fall off.

One day a fancy lady arrived at Anita's house. She looked like a peacock: a very pretty face and fingers covered with shiny rings. The sister of Bartolo from Santiago, people whispered.

"I am Marina from Santiago, Bartolo's sister," she said, looking for Anita. "I want to see Anita so she'll tell me where he's been, what he loved, and what he did."

Anita gave her letters, pictures, and showed her the big stone in the entryway where she used to talk with him. She told her many things, then she called for me.

"Tell the lady that you knew Bartolo," she said, pulling me by the hand.

"Did he love you a lot?" asked the lady whose skirts smelled of flowers. I shook my head. I don't remember if I said yes or no. Taking her by the hand, I led her to the balustrade on the wall of the Hinojos' house, and I showed her the place where he used to sit dangling his legs. "That's where he'd sing. I could see him from this rock."

Anita told Mama, "They've just killed Bartolo over in Chihuahua. He was knocking at her door. Nobody knows who did it, but he was riddled with bullets."

His sister loved him very much. She was very pretty and had many lovers. Bartolo said he was going to kill all the men who kept her company.

Agustín García was tall and light skinned, with a short mustache, fine features, and a sweet expression. He wore leather pants and fur chaps. Slow moving, he didn't seem like a Villista general. When Mama saw him for the first time, she said, "That man is dangerous." He didn't know how to laugh, he spoke very little, and he saw a great deal. He was a friend of Elías Acosta; they drank coffee together. Elías used to laugh and talk, but Agustín García wouldn't say anything. That's how they were different.

One day Mama asked him how Villa's ambush of the Carranzista general, Murguía, had gone. He said they had used hardly any ammunition. "There were lots of *changos*,* and we threw them over the embankments alive." Mama didn't reply. One of those who had died was a boy from our street of Segunda del Rayo.

The general said good-bye, as on other occasions.

At night you could hear a serenade and a voice that seemed familiar singing, "Lovely torrents are the currents that flow from the heart." And later, "I secretly love you. If only you knew." Something startled Mama, who couldn't rest easy after that. Two nights later Mama's fourteen-year-old niece, Irene, showed up at the house very upset. From outside came the noise of a crowd of men. Anxiously, Mama ordered Irene to climb into a fireplace and try to get up to the roof, from where she could get to the house of Doña Rosita, a friend of Mama's who had red hair. They were already circling the house. Mama began to sing in a loud voice. In came a man dragging his spurs, then another and another. "We have orders." They searched all over. Mama said, "Make yourselves at home." They walked in and out. Mama was calm, smoking a cigarette. García entered, tall, very tall, scuffing his feet. In his hand he carried a whip. Everything about him was relaxed. He tapped the whip against his right leg and looked attentively at Mama.

"These are your men," she said.

"They're not mine. I was just passing by and was surprised to see a number of horses here, so I came in."

---

*Slang for "Carranzistas"; also used in Chihuahua to refer to Yaqui Indians. (Trans.)

He sat down, crossed his legs, and began to roll a cigarette. The men saw him, said nothing, and started to leave one by one, without looking back.

"Nothing serious, I hope," he said, laughing.

"Not really," Mama answered calmly, "just soldiers' games."

General Agustín García had intended to carry Irene off, but instead he picked up the guitar and began to sing: "Proud dark-haired girl, I'll not see your face again." And, one foot swinging in the air, he finished a cigarette and a cup of coffee.

His name was Antonio, and he was the leader of the Villa Brigade. He was one of the generals who made the least mischief. Daring and mean-tempered, still he never provoked gossip in Parral or Segunda. Born in San Antonio del Tule, near Balleza, he was tall and swarthy. One of his legs was shorter than the other, and he wore an elevated heel to balance his steps. They told Mama that, after the retreat from Celaya,* during an argument at a station over a horse, he and some other generals got angry, took out their pistols and shot to kill. Several died: Pedro Gutiérrez, about twenty years old, died next to General Silva. General Rodríguez fell under Silva but wasn't killed. That was how Antonio Silva, a man who made quite an impression among the people of Parral, met his end.

"The only commotion concerning Antonio Silva had to do with the sword whippings he used to give men who misbehaved. Back when the troops were quartered up by the Parral station, there was a whipping almost every day. One morning the 'flyers'—men who walked about flapping their elbows as if they were wings—told the general that Alfredo, the most notorious flyer, was expecting a whipping. Silva, who enjoyed nothing in life more than leaving his sword's mark on those fellows, sent for the flyer and told him he was going to do an especially good job on him because he was such a rowdy and a troublemaker."

They say that the prisoner was brought in, pale and trying to appear docile. The general ordered a good whipping. They lowered his pants and tied him against a post. The general raised his sword and began to whip him. "Oh, my God!" said the flyer. "Yes, and all powerful, my son." Thus prayed the flyer, and thus responded the swarthy general. They say that suddenly the sword bent, and Silva said to the flyer, "My sword's worn out already. Go on and pull up your pants and don't go back to your pranks, because one day, if I have to cure you of your tricks again, I'll break this over your ass." Silva used to pace back and forth, stop, turn around, shake his head and gesture with his hands, talking on and on to his men, giving

---

*Celaya, further south in Central Mexico, was the scene in 1915 of two decisive battles between Villa and Obregón that turned the tide of the war in Carranza's favor. Thereafter, Villa and his troops retreated to the North, where, with help from local supporters, fighting continued off and on until 1920. (Trans.)

them advice, because above all he liked order. Then he'd say in a loud voice to his assistant, "Clean the sword and keep it ready in case my boys need a little bare-assed discipline from my holy hand." And he'd continue pacing back and forth, waiting for someone to tell him about more pranks his boys had committed.

Around Segunda del Rayo they liked him a lot, and every time he went by on his rounds they made coffee for him. Once a sentry failed to challenge him with the customary "Who goes there?" and the general told him, "Listen, amigo, when you see me coming, shout the who-goes-there at me, and if I don't answer, fill my hide with lead. Can't you see that I'm just a general and you're the sentry?"

When the news came that Antonio Silva was dead, Mama cried for him. She said it was the end of a real man.

II
THE EXECUTED

He passed by every day, skinny, poorly dressed—a soldier. He became my friend because one day our smiles met. I showed him my dolls, and he smiled. There was hunger in his laughter, and I thought it would be good if I gave him some *gorditas,* thick corn tortillas. The next day, when he went by on his way to the hill, I offered him the *gorditas*. His skinny body smiled and his pale lips spread with a "My name is Rafael. I'm the bugle boy from La Iguana Hill." He clasped the napkin against his frozen stomach and off he went. From behind he looked like a scarecrow. It made me laugh, and I thought he must be wearing a dead man's trousers.

There was a three-day battle in Parral. The fighting was very heavy.

"They're bringing back a dead man," they said, "the only one from La Iguana Hill." He passed by the house on a stretcher made of poplar branches. Four soldiers were carrying him. I stood there speechless, my eyes wide, wide open, I suffered so much. They carried him by. He had several bullet wounds. I saw his trousers—today truly those of a dead man.

Catarino Acosta dressed in black and wore his ten-gallon hat pushed back on his head. Every afternoon he came by the house, greeted Mama by tilting his hat with his left hand, and gave a little smile that, under his black mustache, seemed timid. He had been a Villista, one of Tomás Urbina's colonels back in Las Nieves. Now he was retired and had seven children. His wife, Josefita Rubio, was from Villa Ocampo.

Gudelio Uribe, Catarino's personal enemy, took him prisoner, mounted him on a mule, and paraded him through the streets of Parral. His ears had been cut off, strung together, and hung around his neck. Gudelio was a specialist in cutting people's ears off. Blood dripped from the many wounds in his ribs. Four soldiers on horseback surrounded him as he went along. Whenever they wanted the mule to move faster, they just poked Catarino in the ribs with a bayonet. The prisoner said nothing, his expressionless face was distant. Mama blessed him and cried sorrowfully as he went by.

After persecuting him for a long time, they took him to the blond-haired Uribe. "Here he is, General," the soldiers said, "more dead than alive." They say Uribe treated him very harshly, reminding him of certain incidents in Durango. Then Uribe declared he didn't want to waste even one bullet on killing Catarino. They took his shoes off and led him into the middle of the road with orders to make him run alongside the mounted soldiers until he fell dead from exhaustion. No one was permitted to approach him or use a bullet to put him out of his misery. Orders were given to shoot anyone who might make that gesture of compassion.

Catarino Acosta lasted eight days lying in the road. The crows had already begun to eat him when they finally let his remains be carted off. By the time Villa arrived, Uribe and his generals had already fled from Parral.

They executed Catarino without bullets.

The firing squad knew he was a dangerous prisoner. They kept an eye on his every move. He wore a green suit and a charro hat. A group of twenty or thirty men stood in front of him—strange types, some really quite young and others with white beards. He was a slim, dark, and very restless man.

An unusual execution.

After talking a long time with his general staff, Maclovio Herrera announced to the public that Epifanio had to die because he was a traitor, because he deceived the people by taking their sons and fathers away, hurting both Villa and Carranza. Herrera railed on against the accused who, standing in front of the cemetery wall and facing a firing squad, raised his hat aloft, stood up straight, and said that he was dying for a cause different from the revolution and that he was the worker's friend. He said other things in queer words that no one recalls. In the first volley, only one shot wounded him. Holding his side and leaning against the wall, he said, "Finish me off, you dogs." Another volley, and he fell clutching his hat so tightly that no one was able to remove it to give him the coup de grace. They did it through his hat, putting out one of his eyes.

The people walked back toward their houses. Epifanio's supporters carried away all the objects the dead man had left to them.

He said he was the worker's friend.

Two Mayo friends of mine, Indians from San Pablo de Balleza. They didn't speak Spanish but made themselves understood through sign language. They were fair skinned, with blue eyes and long hair, and they wore big heavy shoes that looked as though they weighed ten kilos. They used to go by the house every day, and I would startle them by squirting streams of water at them with a big syringe, like those used to treat horses. I laughed at how their hair would fly when they ran off. Their shoes looked like two big houses awkwardly dragged along.

One cold, cold morning I was told as I left my house, "Hey, they've executed Zequiel and his brother. They're lying up there outside the cemetery, and no one's left in the soldiers' barracks."

My heart didn't leap, nor was I frightened or even curious, but I started to run. I found them next to one another. Zequiel face down and his brother looking at the sky. Their eyes were wide open, very blue and clouded over, as if they had been crying. I couldn't ask them anything. I counted the bullet wounds, turned Zequiel's head around, cleaned the dirt from the right side of his face, which rather upset me, and in my heart said three or more times, "*Pobrecitos, pobrecitos,* poor things." Their blood had frozen. I gathered it up and put it in the pocket of one of their blue-tassled jackets. It was like little red crystals that would never again turn into warm threads of blood.

I saw their shoes, covered with dust. They no longer looked like houses to me. Today they were hunks of black leather that could tell me nothing about my friends.

I broke the syringe.

They were on the corner of the second street of El Rayo, laughing and talking with a young girl. One of the two boys absentmindedly leaned against a post and covered a notice with his hand. A soldier from De Jesús Barracks saw them, arrested them, and gave them a good whipping. Just then, Miguel Baca Valles appeared and thought to ask the boys, "Where do you come from?" They were cousins from Villa Ocampo, Durango, the younger one the son of José Antonio Arciniega. "Ah! So you're José Antonio's son! I'm going to take you two for a little stroll to the cemetery," said Baca Valles, breaking into a broad grin.

They took them away and, according to the soldiers, shot them both. Apparently the younger one died very bravely; when they were about to open fire, he raised his sombrero and looked toward heaven. Othón died a little fearfully. They weren't put in coffins, just thrown into a grave.

Many strings were pulled to try to disinter them, to no avail. All the locks on the furniture in José Antonio's house had to be broken into because his boy was carrying the key ring and other valuables in the pocket of his vest. Baca Valles, scrupulously considerate, had forbidden anyone to plunder the corpses of the boys from Villa Ocampo.

• *Nacha Ceniceros* •

A large Villista encampment at station *X* near Chihuahua. All was quiet and Nacha was crying. She was in love with a young colonel from Durango by the name of Gallardo. Nacha was a *coronela* who carried a pistol and wore braids. She had been crying after an old woman gave her advice. She went to her tent where she was busily cleaning her pistol when, all of a sudden, it went off.

In the next tent was Gallardo, sitting at a table and talking to a woman. The bullet that escaped from Nacha's gun struck Gallardo in the head and he fell dead.

"Gallardito has been killed, General."

Shocked, Villa replied, "Execute the man who did it."

"It was a woman, General."

"Execute her."

"Nacha Ceniceros."

"Execute her."

She wept for her lover, put her arms over her head, with her black braids hanging down, and met the firing squad's volley.

She made a handsome figure, unforgettable for everyone who saw the execution. Today there is an anthill where they say she was buried.

This was the version that was told for many years in the North of Mexico. The truth came out some time later. Nacha Ceniceros was still alive. She had gone back to her home in Catarinas, undoubtedly disillusioned by the attitude of those few who tried to divide among themselves the triumphs of the majority.

Nacha Ceniceros tamed ponies and rode horses better than many men. She was what's called a country girl, but in the mountain style. With her incredible skill, she could do anything a man could with his masculine strength. She joined the revolution because Porfirio Díaz's henchmen had assassinated her father. If she had wanted to, she could have married one of the most prominent Villista generals. She could have been one of the most famous women of the revolution. But Nacha Ceniceros returned quietly to her ravaged home and began to rebuild the walls and fill in the openings through which thousands of bullets had been fired against the murderous Carranzistas.

The curtain of lies against General Villa, spread by organized groups of slanderers and propagators of the black legend, will fall, just as will the bronze statues that have been erected with their contributions. Now I say—and I say it with the voice of someone who has known how to unravel lies, *Viva Nacha Ceniceros, Coronela de la revolución!*

They were killed quickly, like unpleasant things not meant for public knowledge.

The Portillo brothers, young revolutionaries, why were they killed? According to the graveyard keeper, "Luis Herrera's eyes were red, very red, it looked like he cried blood." Juanito Amparán can't forget them. "It looked like he cried blood."

Luis Herrera brought the Portillo boys to the graveyard one quiet afternoon, unrecorded in the history of the revolution. It was five o'clock.

Elegant, nervous Gerardo Ruiz pointed with a studied smile to the fourteen wounds that studded his chest. When they told him he was going to be executed, he became furious, and his dignified appearance disintegrated before the muzzles of sixteen rifles streaked with grime.

"You can't execute me just on account of those papers," he shouted with all the strength in his feeble lungs. "I am a gentleman, and I cannot die like a thief. You miserable bandits, why am I being shot? I refuse to go! Uncivilized animals, bandits, bandits! What am I a Villista for? I won't go! You listen to me, you miserable old man"—referring to the commanding general, Gorgonio Beltrán—"the Carranzistas didn't give that money to me. It was mine, mine, mine!" And he pounded his chest. "Me? Die for some filthy papers? No, no!" He shouted and carried on for about two hours. The Villista general who ordered him executed listened to all the insults without getting up or blinking an eye. He just sat there twisting his mustache.

"Take him away, now that he's vented his rage, and shoot him," he said in a soft, indifferent voice. His attention was focused on his mustache, which he fingered with the measured rhythm of an absentminded old man.

Since the prisoner was dangerous, they doubled his escort. He refused to walk in the middle of the street because he said he wasn't a bandit. He walked along the sidewalk, furious, cursing the soldiers and their officer. He had walked from the post office to San Francisco Street when he grabbed a rifle from one of the soldiers, whirled around with it and, just as he was about to fire, the rifle jammed. In a matter of seconds, a rain of about twenty bullets fell on his agile, nervous body, which absorbed sixteen of them, yet stayed alive. A 30-30 fired the coup de grace, shooting off one of his ears. His blood was black, said the soldiers, because he died in a rage. Many people saw this execution. It was midday. Mama witnessed everything.

A horseman came around the corner of San Francisco Street, opposite the Hidalgo Theater, dangling in his swarthy, filthy hand a white paper that held captive the life of Gerardo Ruiz. They picked up the body and put it on a squalid, woundingly filthy stretcher. With his foot, someone shoved a little piece of red flesh toward one of the soldiers. "You forgot the ear," he said, laughing at the stupidity of the 30-30s. They picked it up and placed it next to the dead man's face. The rider, with the man's life in his hand, went back to the barracks and put it on a desk.

I thought it was wonderful to see so many soldiers. Men on horseback with lots of cartridge belts, rifles, machine guns, all looking for the same thing: food. They were sick of eating unsalted meat. Before heading off to the mountains in pursuit of Villa, they wanted their fill of frijoles or some other cooked food.

"We're going to bring back Villa's head!" shouted the bands of cavalrymen as they rode through the streets.

A woman appeared at her door and shouted to one of the officers, "Hey, you son of a bitch, bring me back a little bone from Villa's wounded knee so I can make a shrine for it."*

Men here, there and everywhere. A hodgepodge of people. My goodness, how many men, how many people there are in the world, said my child's mind.

One of my aunts came to see Mama and told her that a Yaqui soldier had tried to abduct my cousin Luisa. She talked for a long time, and then the two of them left in a gray automobile. When they returned they were full of chatter, recounting details I can't remember anymore about how the Carranzista general, Pancho Murguía, had received them. My aunt was tickled to death because they had promised her to execute the soldier. She asked eagerly for a cup of coffee.

"How well behaved those *changos* are!" she said to Mama. "They don't even look like generals! Of course, offering to kill the fellow is only meant as a warning to the troops," she said, savoring her coffee. "I'll never forget as long as I live the fright that evil man gave me when he tried to steal my little girl," she assured us, convinced of her suffering.

The next day, as Murguía's troops were leaving town by way of the cemetery, they singled out soldier X from X regiment. He had never laid eyes on my cousin Luisa, but the troops were told, "This man will die for having tried to kiss a young girl."

The man was a Yaqui Indian who spoke no Spanish. He died for a kiss the officer gallantly awarded him.

A terrible frigid spell had descended. The people, chilled to the bone, said distractedly, "They killed a *chango* (they also called Yaquis that in Chihuahua). The wind replied, "One less for Villa to gobble up."

I think my aunt gave a coquettish smile to the *changos*' general.

---

*Villa was wounded in the knee on 29 March 1916 in the first encounter between his units and the U.S. expeditionary force under General John J. Pershing, sent to pursue Villa after his raid on Columbus, New Mexico, earlier that month. (Trans.)

The Heart of Colonel Bufanda
(A Carranzista who ordered the slaughter
of an unarmed barracks.)

Colonel Bufanda's hand was stiff from throwing grenades. The unarmed barracks were those of El Aguila and Las Carolinas. The assault left more than three hundred dead in El Aguila alone. The colonel came out with his hand numb.

Right in the middle of the street, someone—no one knew who—fired a shot that hit him near the left shoulder blade and exited through the pouch of his jacket, pushing his heart out with it.

"That expanding bullet was well spent," said the men who passed by.

A woman doctor who lived next to El Aguila Barracks took the dead man into her house. She had already laid him out when Rosalío Hernández's men arrived, dragged him out of the house, and threw him into the middle of the street where his shattered skull lay clinging to the rocks. His face had a look of satisfaction on it.

The pouch of his jacket, the left pouch, shredded like a rose, said my eyes, taking their bearings from the voice of the cannon.

Bufanda gave his best smile to those who were breaking camp. Everyone despised him, and they all gave him kicks. He kept on smiling.

Babis sold candies in the window of a Japanese store. Babis laughed and his eyes closed. He was my friend. He used to give me tons of candy. He told me that he loved me because I knew how to fight with the boys who threw stones. He couldn't fight—not out of fear, but because he was already a grown man. "I've seen big fellows fight over by Mercaderes Street, near the river," he said. "I don't like stones as much as bullets. When I'm called up for service"—and he squinted his eyes, jutting out his teeth—"I'm going to fight real good." And he gave me a handful of caramels. Every day he would tell me he was about to go off with a troop, and he especially liked green trousers. "I'm going to buy myself some chaps with silver buckles," he chanted like a song. And I, very serious, said to him, "But they're going to kill you. I know they're going to kill you. It's written on your face." He laughed and gave me some big sugarplums. I told Mama what Babis said to me. I was awfully sad.

One day I found the candies unattended. Babis must have been wearing green trousers and soldier's buttons. How eager I was to see him! He probably looked like a prince.

A month passed—like a year to my yellow eyes—without seeing Babis. A soldier coming from Jiménez sought out our house. He had something to tell Mama. He arrived unannounced. "Braulio, the one who used to work in New Japan on Ojito Street, had gone off with them. He was a scared fellow." That's what the soldier said, standing by the trolley track with his hands in his pockets. (I wanted to pounce on him when I heard that. Babis wasn't scared. He used to steal candies to give me.) "During the battle for Jiménez, Babis was among the first prisoners to be taken. They burned up the prisoners with gasoline. It's the way these days. That's how Babis died in the first battle." Without having his silver buckles, I think. The man, rocking on one foot, said the screams of the prisoners being burned alive still rang in his ears. They were loud. Later, they gradually grew fainter.

The soldier made a strange gesture with his right hand and headed up the street, walking between the trolley tracks, swaying from side to side, and carrying Babis' screams in his ears.

The firing had begun at four in the morning. It was ten o'clock. They said that El Kirilí and others were the ones who were at the corner of Tita alley "having at it" with some Carranzistas who had taken shelter on the other side of the street. The truth is the bullets, flying right by our door, seemed lots of fun to me. Right then, I wanted to stick my head out to see how El Kirilí was fighting. Mama told Felipe Reyes, a boy from Las Cuevas, to watch us and not let us go out. We girls were eager to see the men fall. We imagined the street strewn with bodies. The firing continued, though somewhat abated. Felipe entertained himself playing with some tools, and my sister and I climbed up to peer out a window, our eyes wide in anticipation. Looking all around, we didn't see a single body, which we really regretted. We had to content ourselves with the glimpse of an occasional round of fire coming from the corner, and every now and then, a hat raised up on the tip of a rifle.

Suddenly, from El Kirilí's corner, a man came out on horseback. Before long, he was in front of our house, and we could see he was missing a leg and carrying a crutch across his saddle. He was pale, with a nice face, and a nose like the blade of a sword. He thought he saw a group of men in gray, further up the street, signaling to him. He didn't look back or anything, just rode along as if hypnotized by those people. No bullets were being fired at that moment.

"Look how yellow he is," said my sister with a squeal that made me remember Felipe Reyes.

"He's really white from the fear of dying," I said, convinced of my knowledge in matters of death.

Two seconds later he reached Ojito Street and disappeared. The men began to fire again at the corner of Tita, louder than ever. All of this happened in an instant, at most, three minutes. Felipe dragged us away from the window.

Then the firing stopped. All the people came out of their houses, anxious to see who had "gotten it." Not many of the dead were known in that area, a few Carranzistas in gray blankets, very grimy and unshaven.

El Mochito ("the Maimed One"), with his uniform all done up, gold buttons sparkling in the sun, lay very rigid, as if giving a military salute. His saddlebag was turned inside out, his eyes half open, and his one shoe, perforated by two bullets, lay next to his face. They say that when he had already fallen, they gave him two coups de grace, first placing the shoe on his face (he had two little spots on him, one between the eyebrows and another higher up, but with no powder burns). They said they put the shoe on him so that his *tontas*—an adjective used for sweethearts—wouldn't see him disfigured.

Nonetheless, that body with bullets in it had left this life. The maimed man, who passed by our house, was already dead.

"José Díaz is the handsomest, most elegant and distinguished fellow I know. He promised to come over for coffee," said Papa's sister, Toña.

"Toña likes *macuchi* tobacco and isn't ashamed to be seen rolling her own cigarettes. Mama's cigarettes are factory made. Mama likes coffee, and I think that's why I do too. Mama is prettier than Toña," I thought to myself, bringing to an end my profound and tiring meditations.

Handsome José Díaz was talking. Three times I said to myself, "Yes, I'm going to make him Pitaflorida's beau. (Pitaflorida was my doll princess.) I'll make her a blue dress and I'll put honest-to-goodness stars on it—the kind Don Luis, the notions man, sells." (I spoke very softly, closing my eyes.) José Díaz stopped by the house regularly. He wore a glittering sword and gold and silver buttons—or so they seemed to my child's eyes. He'd join the band in *gallos*, or serenades, on nights that were very dark or when there was a full moon. All the girls of Segunda del Rayo fell in love with José. He wore a different outfit every day and rode around town in a red car. One day he told Toña that he hated the sun because it was bad for his face and hands. She thought that was very nice, and I (whom they called "sunlover") thought it was just fine, on account of Pitaflorida. I would never dream of marrying my princess to a swarthy type.

Then he stopped visiting, but many afternoons he'd pass by the house. I used to sit Pitaflorida in the window so she could see him, and when I dressed her, I'd tell her the things he said. My doll was very moved.

When she heard the car go by, Toña would peek through the foyer door. My doll was the only girl who didn't hide to look at him. Sometimes he'd laugh when he passed by the house. Pitaflorida didn't laugh.

There was a seven-hour battle, with the Villistas surrounded. The fighting was fierce. One group of cavalry left by way of Los Aburridos Hill, straight for the Rubio ranch.

No, no! He was never the beau of Pitaflorida, my doll, who broke her head when she fell out the window. She never laughed with him.

Young, handsome José Díaz died devoured by grime. He got his bullet wounds so he wouldn't hate the sun.

The Sentinel of El Aguila Barracks

El Aguila Barracks is wide, flat, dirty inside and out. It has the look of an animal stretching out its front paws with its snout open. Part of the Chao Brigade, disarmed the night before, was sleeping. The threads of the soldiers' lives were held by the sentinel's eyes. In his filthy hands, warm from eating, a rifle with five rusty cartridges. He was standing by a large boulder—a northerner, tall, in a jacket with sleeves too short—and the blades of his breath cut the night air as he tried to be ghostlike. He didn't hear the noise of the Carranzistas who were two yards away, dragging themselves along the ground. The bullet hit him in the left temple, and he died standing up. His body lay stretched out there next to the boulder. Very straight, without shoes now, his mouth half open, his eyes closed. He was a pretty dead man in his new pose, with his hands crossed. Some looked at him spitefully. "He didn't sound the warning." Inside the barracks were three hundred bodies scattered around the patio, in the stables, in the rooms. In every corner were small groups of bullet-ridden bodies, half-sitting, lying across the doorways, along the edge of walkways. Their faces, spattered with blood, had the desperate look of men who die by surprise. (A little eight-year-old boy, Roberto Rendón, dressed as a soldier, also died in the patio. He lay on his left side with his arms open, his face sideways on the ground, his bent legs seeming to take a step—his first step as a man.)

As they were leaving the hill, they shot El Chino Ortiz. When my brother, called El Siete, saw him holding his stomach and falling off his horse, he ran to him, "What direction did the bullets come from, Chino?" El Siete said he could barely get out, "From the hill of La Cruz."

The Guanajuato Barracks was the only one still returning fire. The Carranzistas, hiding on the roofs of the houses across the way, were trying to make them surrender. Just then, the soldiers of Rosalío Hernández—who, the day before leaving Parral, halted their trains on account of the rain—advanced in lines of sharpshooters until they reached the trapped Guanajuatans, overrunning the enemy and saving the barracks.

Mama went out to look for her thirteen-year-old son. I stuck close to her skirts. Next to the Guanajuato bridge was a young lad clinging to a horse. "That's him," I said running. "El Siete really loves his horse." When Mama turned him around, we saw that he was someone else. His eyes were wide open and his hands dug into the horse. I don't think he had a mother.

We went on. When we got to Juárez Plaza, in the area of Guanajuato, we saw some charred bodies under a kiosk. They were burned to a crisp and black, very black. One had his head between his knees. To our left we saw the valiant barracks building, pockmarked with bullets. The sidewalk strewn with Carranzista bodies. You could recognize them by their filthy clothes. They had come from the mountains and hadn't bathed in many months. We went through an alleyway leading to El Aguila Barracks—it smelled of urine and was so narrow it made our feet sad—but when we saw a body wedged against the wall we began to run. He was lying face down, hair all rumpled and dirty, hands broad and brown, the nails black. A gray sarape was folded over his shoulder. He was smothered in grime and my heart cringed to see him. "In this ugly alleyway!" I said when I saw his face. I was shocked. José Díaz, the one with the red car, the beau of all the ladies of Segunda del Rayo, the one Toña cried over!

"More than three hundred men shot all at once, inside a barracks, is really extraordinary," the people said, but our young eyes found it quite natural.

As we left the building, we saw the sentinel again. No one knew his name. Some said he had fired a shot; others said no. I know the young sentinel didn't die next to the large boulder. He was already a ghost. He had five rusty cartridges in his hands and a pose that was a treat to our eyes.

A tall man with a blond mustache. He spoke forcefully. He had come into the house with ten men, and was insulting Mama, saying, "Do you claim you're not a Villa partisan? Do you deny that? There are firearms here. If you don't give them to us, along with the money and the ammunition, I'll burn down your house!" He spoke walking back and forth in front of her. Lauro Ruiz (from the town of Balleza) was the name of another man with him. They all shoved and bullied us. The man with the blond mustache was about to hit Mama, then he said, "Tear the place apart. Look everywhere."

They poked their bayonets into everything, pushing my little brothers and sisters toward Mama, but he wouldn't allow us to get close to her. I rebelled and went over to her, but he gave me a shove and I fell down. Mama didn't cry. She told them to do what they pleased but not to touch her children. Even with a machine gun, she couldn't have fought them all. The soldiers stepped on my brothers and sisters and broke everything. Since they didn't find firearms, they carried off what they wanted, and the blond man said, "If you complain, I'll come and burn your house down." Mama's eyes, grown large with revolt, did not cry. They had hardened, reloaded in the rifle barrel of her memory.

I have never forgotten the picture of my mother, back up against the wall, eyes fixed on the black table, listening to the insults. That blond man, too, has been engraved in my memory ever since.

Two years later, we went to live in Chihuahua. I saw him going up the steps of the Government Palace. He had a smaller mustache then. That day everything was ruined for me: I couldn't study, I spent it thinking about being a man, having my own pistol and firing a hundred shots into him.

Another time, he was with some people in one of the windows of the Palace, laughing with his mouth open and his mustache shaking. I don't want to say what I saw him do, nor what he said, because it would seem an exaggeration. Again I dreamed of having a pistol.

One day, here in Mexico City, I saw a photograph in a newspaper with this caption: "General Alfredo Rueda Quijano, before a summary court-martial." It was the same blond man (his mustache was even smaller). Mama was no longer with us. Without being sick, she closed her eyes one day and remained asleep, back in Chihuahua.* (I know Mama was tired of hearing the 30-30s.) Today they were going to shoot him, here in the capital. The people felt sorry for him, admired him, and made a great scene over his death, so he could shout out loud, just as he shouted at Mama the night of the attack.

The soldiers who fired at him had taken hold of my pistol with a hundred shots.

All night long, I kept saying to myself, "They killed him because he abused Mama, because he was bad to her." Mama's hardened eyes were mine now, and I repeated, "He was bad to Mama. That's why they shot him."

When I saw his picture on the front page of the Mexico City newspapers, I sent a child's smile to those soldiers who held in their hands my pistol with its hundred bullets, turned into a carbine resting against their shoulders.

* Rafaela Luna died in 1923. (Trans.)

General Sobarzo's Guts

About three in the afternoon, we were by the big rock on San Francisco Street. As we went down La Pila de Don Cirilo Reyes alleyway, we saw some soldiers coming our way, carrying a tray above their heads, talking and laughing. "Hey, what's that pretty thing you're carrying?" From up the street we had been able to see that there was something pretty and red in the basin. The soldiers smiled at each other, lowered the tray, and showed it to us. "They're guts," said the youngest one, fixing his eyes on the two of us to see if we were frightened. When we heard "they're guts," we moved up close to see them. They were all rolled together, as if they had no end. "Guts! How nice! Whose are they?" we said, our curiosity showing in our eyes. "They belong to General Sobarzo," said the same soldier. "We're taking them to be buried in the cemetery." And off they went, all in step, without another word. We told Mama that we'd seen Sobarzo's guts. She had seen them too going along the iron bridge.

I don't remember if they were on the attack for five days, but that time the Villistas weren't able to take the plaza. I believe the commanding officer's name was Luis Manuel Sobarzo and that he was killed near La Cruz Hill or near the station. He was from Sonora. They embalmed him and put him on a train. His guts stayed in Parral.

The man whose hand was sticking out the train window—bruised and with nails so black it looked strangled—was talking so fervently that the *macuchi* cigarette behind his ear kept moving and looked like it would fall to the floor. I was hoping to see it fall. "Machines, land, plows, nothing but machinery and more machinery!" he said with his arms open, his ideas swaying with the movement of the coach. "The government doesn't understand. It doesn't see." No one answered him. When the water vendor came by, everyone asked for a bottle. They offered him one. "No, I never drink water. My whole life, coffee, only coffee. Water tastes bad to me," he said, clearing his throat. "When we get to Camargo, I'll have my coffee."

He spoke in ten different tones of voice, always asking some phantom for the same thing: machinery.

In Santa Rosalía de Camargo Sandías, everyone was eating watermelon. My freckled nose was buried in a slice Mama gave me when, suddenly, we saw a bunch of men on horseback next to a telegraph post, trying to throw a rope over it. When they succeeded, they handed the end to one man, who jammed his spurs into his horse. The horse leaped into motion. On the other end was the man they were hanging. The one on horseback stopped at a certain distance, when the rope was taut, and looked toward the post as if trying to read an advertisement from far away. Then he moved back little by little until the hanged man was at the right height. The others cut the rope, and they all rode off, carrying along a cloud of dust in their horses' hooves. Mama said nothing, but she stopped eating the watermelon. The seat opposite us was vacant. The man who dangled his hand out the window was hanging in front of the train, not ten meters from where we were. The *macuchi* cigarette had fallen from his ear, and the hanged man looked as though he was searching for it with his tongue. Slowly the train pulled out of the station, leaving behind, swinging from a post, the man who drank coffee all his life.

A window two meters above a street corner. Two girls looking down on a group of ten men with their weapons drawn, aiming at a young man on his knees, unshaven and grimy, who was begging desperately. Terribly sick, he writhed in terror, stretching out his hands toward the soldiers. He was dying of fear. The officer next to them was giving signals with his sword. When he raised it, as if to stab the sky, ten bursts of fire left the 30-30s and embedded themselves in the young man's body, swollen with alcohol and cowardice. Lifted into the air by the shots, he then fell, blood pouring out of him through many holes. His hands stayed clapped over his mouth. There he lay for three days. One afternoon, somebody or other carried him away.

Since he lay there for three nights, I became accustomed to seeing the scrawl of his body, fallen toward the left with his hands on his face, sleeping there, next to me. That dead man seemed mine. There were moments when, fearful he would be taken away, I would get up and run to the window. He was my obsession at night. I liked to look at him because I thought he was very afraid.

One day, after dinner, I went running to see him from the window, but he wasn't there anymore. Someone had stolen the timid dead man. The ground remained marked and desolate. That night I went to sleep dreaming they would shoot someone else and hoping it would be next to my house.

They told Mama everything that had happened. She never forgot it. Those men had been her *paisanos*.

"It happened in Nieves," said Mama, "at the Urbina hacienda. Isidro (El Kirilí) was there. The Villistas burst in shooting and surprised them. They were only a few, and most were killed. General Urbina was wounded and taken prisoner. Later they set off for Rosario with him, but never arrived. Urbina was killed. The night was so dark it seemed like a wolf's mouth. They said General Villa was quite surprised to hear of the death of his *compadre* Urbina, but everyone knew that Fierro had told him Urbina was preparing to go over to the enemy and that he had no choice but to intervene with bullets." Mama said it was all due to a hunch of Villa's.

"Urbina's troops came to Parral," Mama said, "and it was just dreadful, the men all so angry their faces were contorted with rage. From one end of town to the other, they made inquiries everywhere, hoping to find their leader. They didn't believe he could be dead. No one knew it for a fact, but they guessed it.

"There were many executions, and they were all my *paisanos*," said Mama, her voice sad and eyes filled with pain. "They wanted people to sign up, to declare themselves Villistas, and if not, they executed them. Most of the officers were shot. All the generals acknowledged Villa as their jefe—just a signature and they were saved—but Santos Ruiz wouldn't do it. Santos was a native of my region, very young, around twenty-four, and a brave general." Mama's voice trembled when she said that he was a soldier of the revolution and a native of her region. "There was a strong feeling against executing him. Santos had told them he didn't want to be a Villista. No one wanted to shoot him, even the staunchest Villistas pleaded for his life and had hopes of convincing him. They gave him plenty to drink, but not even sotol could get him to sign. One day they put him in jail to see if that would make him come to his senses, as they said. Then all his relatives arrived. Fidelina, Santos' sister who loved him a lot, went to the jail every day and asked the general, Santos Ortiz, to spare her brother's life. One morning, on the general's order, they stopped letting her in to see him. Many things happened to that man," Mama said, with memory between her lips. "When he had been locked up for fifteen days, one of his companions, who was an intimate friend and was also going to die with him, of his own choice, said to him, 'You look sad, as if you were sick. Why don't you shave, Santos, you could use it.' And the young general answered, 'They're about to kill me, and I want to finish this novel.' They didn't know when—in an hour, several days—they only knew they would be killed because they had condemned themselves.

"I sent them two or three books," said Mama, very anxious to tell the tragedy of that brave man. "I thought they might amuse themselves reading. No one believed they would be killed. We even thought they had been forgotten about, until the day Fidelina came running out of Tita's house crying, 'They're killing my brother, they're killing my brother.'" Mama said it made her very sad that Fidelina was so distraught and desperate; it hurt to see her. (I think her dark figure must have been striking, but since she had braids, they must have danced in the air, more resigned than she, and looked prettier.) She went back inside the house and then ran out again. Three muffled shots were heard from the direction of the jail. It was around one o'clock in the afternoon. "May God remember the hour," said Mama, full of grief. No shooting was as vivid in her memory as this one; for no one else did she feel such pain. "I heard the shots from the door of Reyes' carpentry shop, and I put my hand to my chest. My head was throbbing. I too ran, not knowing what to do. Then, when I heard the coups de grace, I stopped short and turned back, crying. They had killed a *paisano* of mine. There was nothing anyone could do to help him." Mama dried her tears, awfully hurt inside. (My eyes were wide open, and my thoughts raced in search of images of dead men, men who had been executed. I liked hearing those tragic stories. It seemed to me I could see and hear everything. I needed to have those terrifying pictures in my child's soul. I only regretted that it made Mama's eyes fill with tears to tell them. She suffered a great deal witnessing those horrors. Her beloved people were falling. She saw them and wept for them.) "Later, they brought the boxes, three boxes, and placed them in the big sitting room. They wanted everything to look very elegant. Why? I asked myself, if Santos is no longer alive. The boxes had handles that looked like silver, and they put big candlesticks around them. Santos lay in the middle, surrounded by the other two who died for the pleasure of being his friends and so he wouldn't go alone. I saw those boxes," said her voice, "and those big tapers, and I could still hear the muffled shots, as if from inside a jar. Fidelina told me that, two hours before he died, Santos shaved and told them he was doing it so his sister wouldn't see him looking ugly. 'They'll see me clean-shaven, and my sister will forgive me.' As he faced the soldiers who were going to shoot him, he asked them not to fire at his face, and he told them how they should administer the coup de grace. He directed them to return the books and said that *The Three Musketeers* was the one he had liked best. Poor Santos Ruiz," exclaimed Mama with tears in her eyes.

"May God preserve him in heaven." (And after that, her voice became inaudible, because, I think, she was praying for Santos Ruiz.) Other times, when she was recounting something, she would suddenly turn quiet, unable to continue. Telling about the end of her people was all she had left. I would listen to her, not moving my eyes or my hands. Many times, I edged closer to hear her conversations, without her noticing me.

One day she took me by the hand and walked with me to the house of my godmother, a very pretty lady with green eyes, blond hair and a boyfriend. We turned at San Nicolás, went by Las Carolinas, and stopped at a small open field. I didn't question her as she led me along, saying, "I'm going to show my daughter something." She looked around carefully, and we kept going. "Here it was," she said, stopping by a blue stone. "Look here," she said to me. "This was the spot where a man died. He was our countryman. José Beltrán. He kept firing on them until the last moment. They riddled him with bullets. Here's where it happened. Even down on his knees, as God taught him, he fired at them and reloaded his rifle. He took on a lot of them. He had been tracked down and followed to this spot. He was eighteen years old." She couldn't go on. We left the stone, and Mama didn't say another word. I turned to look at her face, while following along beside her. My eyes came to rest on her slender nose. When we were about to arrive at my godmother's, Mama said to me, "You must kiss my *comadre*'s hand. She is your godmother, your second mother."

Mama told her she had just come from seeing the place where José Beltrán had died. My godmother said something back to her. Later they talked and drank coffee. I saw the place where José Beltrán died. I didn't know why, or when, but I would never forget it.

El Peet said that everything was very strange that night. A lot of troops arrived from Chihuahua, pushing and shoving each other in the streets. Parral is a quiet town at night. Its streetlights look like a poor man's shirt buttons. With Villista cavalry everywhere, the streets were full to overflowing. No one was surprised, but the lampposts were question marks.

In what part of the Northern Division was Villa with his Stetson pulled down to his eyes? No one knew.

El Peet told Mama, "Now they've all left. We just shot Fierro's driver, who told us quite a lot on our way here; he said, 'General Fierro ordered me shot because the car took a bounce and he hit his head on one of the roof beams. He cursed me up and down, and when I told him I didn't know my way around this town, it was enough to make him order my execution. So that's it, I'm going to die. There's no stopping it. I only ask you to send this envelope to Chihuahua for me, so at least they'll know that I ended up among the mounds of dirt in this cemetery.'"

El Peet said the man spoke with the haste of somebody who wants to settle a sensible matter as quickly as possible, "I don't understand, my friends, why the general didn't stick a bullet in me right then when the car bounced." El Peet said, "Listen, Mama, remember that piece of rail that juts out right down by the station exit? Well, that's what the car banged into. It was the first time the driver had come to town and he didn't know the streets." The accused died uncomplainingly. El Peet said that the fellow didn't have time to get frightened, that he told them all those troops were on their way to Las Nieves to see Urbina and that Villa was traveling among them in disguise and that no one knew why they were going there.

"What makes me sad is that when he fell, still warm, not even dead yet, they pounced on him and cut off his fingers in order to steal two rings, and since he was wearing good clothes, they stripped him bare, not even leaving his pants. If you could see what thieves they are! I feel ashamed of it all," said El Peet, bowing his head in sadness.

The Death of Felipe Angeles*

"They're bringing Felipe Angeles with some other prisoners. They aren't killing them," the people were saying. I thought he must be a general, like almost all the Villistas. The newspaper carried the picture of an old man with white hair, no beard, tennis shoes, wearing ragged clothes and a very sad face. "They will be court-martialed," said the papers. There were three prisoners: Trillito, fourteen years old, Arce, a grown man, and Angeles. My younger brother and I ran to Los Heroes Theater. Somehow we managed to get up close to the stage. Sitting around a table to the right was a circle of men; to the left, another table of men, which I don't remember clearly. Next to it was the representative of the public magistrate, an attorney by the name of Victores Prieto. On the right side of the pit was Diéguez. Seated in the circle was Escobar. By the footlights, near us, were the prisoners: Angeles in the middle, Trillito next to the lights.

The interrogation began from the large table. Something was said about Felipe Angeles. The prisoner got up, hands crossed behind his back. (I'm telling what impressed me most, no longer recalling any of the strange words or names I didn't understand.)

"First of all," said Angeles, "I want to express my thanks to Colonel Otero for his attentions on my behalf. He sent me this suit (a coffee-colored suit that swam on him) so I could be presentable before you." (He lifted his arms so everyone could see how big it was.) No one responded. He continued, "I know you are going to kill me, *you want to kill me*. This is no court-martial. For a court-martial you need this and this, so many generals, so many of this and so many of that," and he counted on his fingers, using big words I don't recall. "It is not my fault they will die too (and he pointed to the other accused men). This youngster, whose only crime is that he came to see me so that I would cure his leg, and this other

---

*General Felipe Angeles, trained as a professional soldier in the federal army, was an exceptional artillery commander and strategist. Highly educated and well read, he became a committed socialist and joined ranks with Villa against Carranza in the hope of turning a peasant guerrilla army into an orderly force for national reconstruction. He was captured by government troops, tried on 24–25 November 1919 in Parral, and executed the next day. (Trans.)

fellow are only guilty of being with me at the time I was arrested. I joined up with Villa because he was my friend. When I went into the mountains with him, it was to appease him. I argued with him, and I succeeded in changing his mind about a lot of things. On one occasion, we argued the whole night. Several times he was ready to take out his pistol. (We were at X ranch.) Dawn found us still at it. Everyone thought I would be dead by then."

One man in spats—I think it was Escobar—asked him, "And do you call it a labor of peace going around ransacking houses and burning towns like you did in Ciudad Juárez?" Angeles shook his head, and the man in spats shouted in a loud voice, "I myself fought against you!"

They talked a great deal. I don't recall what about, but I do remember when Angeles told them they were convened without constituting a real court-martial. This, that, and the other, he said, and he mentioned New York, Mexico, France, and the world. Since he was talking about artillery and cannons, I thought his cannons were named New York, etc. The circle of men listened, listened, listened . . .

Mama got mad at us. She said, "Don't you know they're saying that Villa could have come into the theater at any moment to set Angeles free? The slaughter would have been terrible." We were kept in the house. Now we couldn't go back to hear the man in the coffee-colored suit talk.

After he had been executed, I went with Mama to see him. He wasn't in a coffin. He wore a black suit and had cotton in his ears. His eyes were tightly shut, and his face looked tired, probably from having talked as long as the trial lasted—three days, I think it was. Pepita Chacón talked with Mama. I didn't miss a word she said. The night before, she had gone to see Angeles. He was eating a chicken dinner and was very pleased to see her. They had known each other for years. When he saw the black suit that had been left for him on a chair, he asked, "Who sent this?" Someone told him, "The Revilla family." Slowly sipping his coffee, he said, "Why did they bother? There's no need. I can be buried in this one." When they said good-bye, he said, "Listen, Pepita, how's that lady you introduced me to in your house?" "She died, general, and went to heaven. Please say hello to her for me there." Pepita assured Mama that Angeles, with a gentlemanly smile, replied, "Yes, I'll be most pleased to say hello to her."

Everyone had something to say about that execution. Mama said some even cried for Pablito. She didn't actually see it because she was in Parral. Martín told her all about it. He cried a lot and told her that "he wanted to die just like his brother Pablito, real brave, a real man."

Pablito López had ordered some Americans shot one day. "Don't shoot them," some men told him. "Can't you see they're Americans?"

The young general, laughing to himself like a boy they were trying to scare, said to them, "Well, until we know if they're apples or pears, charge them up to me."

And then and there the Americans were shot.

One day they had gone to Columbus.* Pablo and Martín López got it into their heads to burn down the whole town. Pablo was wounded during the attack. He went into hiding in the mountains. Everyone in the United States railed against him, hated him, and wanted to see him hanged from a tree.

Francisco del Arco, a Carranzista colonel who cut an elegant figure, made a deal with some fellows who turned the wounded man over to him. To all appearances, Colonel del Arco had gone looking for Pablo, despite the risks involved. Not everyone believes that. They say the colonel was a dandy, but they all congratulated him just the same.

So Pablito, leaning on a crutch and a cane, was brought to Chihuahua. He had several wounds, which they wanted to treat, but he wouldn't allow it. "What for? I won't be needing it," he said. He knew they were going to execute him. He didn't complain, said no last words, sent no letters. The morning of his execution, he asked for breakfast. As he drank his coffee, he smoked a cigar. They told him he'd be shot in the center of town, in public view. He smiled. (That's how he looks in the photographs.) Picking up his crutch and leaning on it, he lowered his eyes,

---

*On 9 March 1916 Pancho Villa and his men crossed the border and raided the town of Columbus, New Mexico, evidently in retaliation for U.S. recognition of the Carranza government and U.S. support for Carranza's ally Obregón against Villa. More than one hundred Mexicans and seventeen U.S. citizens died in the fighting. (Trans.)

looked at his wounded legs, and then shyly raised his head as if asking, "Well, shall we get on with it?"

They shot him in front of all the townspeople. (There are a number of pictures of the execution.) As a last wish, he asked not to die in the presence of a certain American among the crowd. "I don't want to die in front of that guy," said the shy young general in no uncertain terms.

The bullets knocked him off his crutch, flat onto the ground. The wounds from Columbus no longer bothered him.

I think Colonel del Arco was the type who probably perfumed his mustache and enjoyed his triumph, right down to the heels of his elegant military boots, and he must have walked away measuring his steps and believing in his own importance.

Tomás Ornelas was on his way from Juárez to Chihuahua, and near Villa Ahumada, at Laguna Station, the train was attacked by General Villa and his people. Ornelas had been one of Villa's trusted officers. He once held the post of commanding general of Ciudad Juárez, but he later turned the city over to the Carranzistas, betraying Villa and stealing plenty for himself. After that, he quietly went off to live in El Paso.

The General always knew what was going on. That's how he found out that Ornelas was traveling that day in the caboose of a train, in hiding and fearful of being seen. When he heard Villa's voice saying to him, "Howdy, friend, did you think we wouldn't meet again in this world?" he got red in the face, tried to climb under the seat, and squirmed like a caged animal.

"How well dressed he is! Look what a nice hat and good shirt he's wearing, from the money he stole! Get him off this train," Villa said to his men, "and strip him!" A voice close to Mama said something about a few bullets well spent. The gray shirt fell next to the train tracks in the middle of the desert. Mama's eyes held the image of the man grasping his shirt as he fell to his knees and gave up his life. Stories saved for me, and I never forgot. Mama carried them in her heart.

Salvador, one of José Rodríguez's men, is from Segunda del Rayo Street. He was born there. He told Mama something about Carlos Almeida, and about the fight with Tomás Rivas. (Tomasito Rivas was also from Segunda del Rayo.) He told her that José had been killed in a double-cross, and José this and José that. He gave her all the details. It so happened that José Rodríguez had been born in Satevó. One day he became a Villista general. Young and brave, he rode a horse well and knew the mountains. In numerous battles and countless fights, José Rodríguez and his strong, stocky men found a way through, leaving their enemies lying behind. He didn't pick fights, he didn't talk much. One day, his chief of staff betrayed him in order to steal the money José carried in his saddlebags. Rodríguez became very sad—very angry, I think—sad enough to shoot himself in the neck. Just as he fired, they tried to grab the pistol away from him.

Later, they sent him to Ciudad Juárez to have his wound treated, but he didn't get there alive. Some American ranchers killed him along the way.

Everyone in Parral wept for José Rodríguez.

The sun was high in the sky. Two bodies lay on view in the middle of town, and everyone went to see them. Some said, "It's Pablo López." "It's Siañez," said others. Nobody knew. Those two dead men were Manuel Baca Valles and José Rodríguez. The enemy claimed they were bandits—that's why they put them on view—but they themselves didn't realize that the big tall one was José Rodríguez, commander of the Villista cavalry, right arm of Francisco Villa. They were satisfied saying, "They're a couple of thieves." How stupid the Carranzistas were! They didn't know their business. They could have written: Rodríguez, Villista cavalry, commander, etc.

Laughing to himself, José Rodríguez was probably saying to them in a friendly voice, "Anyway, fellows, let me rest a bit in the sun, lying here in front of the people." (But he didn't say it, because José was actually mocking them.)

They had been set out on a platform for all the people of Ciudad Juárez to see.

His father said, "My José, my son José, how big and strong he was! Twenty years old, and they killed him. When they brought me the news, I went up to the mountains and cried."

My great-uncle knew him well. "What they say about El Chapo is all lies," he said. "El Chapo was a real man of the revolution. These know-it-alls today, who try to make a saint of him, never even met him!" And he narrates, as if it were a story, "General Tomás Urbina was born in Nieves, Durango, the eighteenth day of August of the year 1877."

Before the Revolution, he was a stableboy who had a pistol, a lasso, and a horse. The mountains, sotol, and the rural police made him the man he was.

His mother, Doña Refugio, would anxiously wait up for him. She prayed to the Blessed Infant of Atocha, and he watched over him. A man who crosses the mountains must travel armed and be prepared to kill. Tomás' panorama was the same as all the others. Men of the countryside: feared face to face and shot in the back.

Urbina wore tight-fitting, black cloth pants, a cowboy shirt, and a large sombrero. Few years on his bones covered with dark skin. He knew how to break in ponies, lasso animals and men. He liked to drink brandy and sleep entwined in the black tresses of some woman (a combination he hid from my great-uncle).

The revolution and his friendship with Pancho Villa made him a soldier of the revolution, watched over by the Blessed Infant of Atocha.

He got to be a general because he knew how to deal with men and animals. He got to be a general because he knew about gunfire and how to think with his heart.

Urbina, the general, failed Urbina, the man.

In those days he was in Ebano, traveling toward Celaya. Back in Nieves some personal matters occurred that, when he got word of them, wiped the general's smile from his face. His brother, Margarito, knew all about it: *Doña María and the chief of the harness makers of the Morelos Brigade.*

Urbina, with the star on his sombrero, his thick veins pulsing under his swarthy skin, and his eyes bulging out of his head like an athlete's, gave a general's snort when he got that news. (This is just innocent guesswork, thought up today, here where people know nothing of the Blessed Infant of Atocha and General Tomás Urbina.)

Urbina gave his brother the order to go to Villa Ocampo and have Catarino Acosta immediately shoot the harness maker on Doña María's doorstep. The order was carried out. She lifted him up and took him into her house, right to the room where Urbina had set up a permanent shrine to the Blessed Infant of Atocha, with lighted candles, to the very spot where she slept and prayed. Nobody else ever went into that room. Doña María lay the dead man down there. She kept watch over his body and had him buried.

Back in Ebano, Urbina learned of this, and it undid him completely. His emotions exploded.

Three people tell the rest of the story. Rodolfo Fierro's troops went by between six and ten at night on their way to Las Nievas. What day was it? What month? What year? They were in a big hurry and kept their voices down. Shortly after arriving, they shot Fierro's driver, who had told them, while they were taking him to the cemetery, that Villa was thereabouts, in disguise, but no one knew what his plan was.

El Kirilí was with Tomás Urbina at his hacienda, and he said that when the first shots were fired, they began to stand wool mattresses up in front of the door. That was when El Kirilí's finger was shot off, no doubt the finger on which he wore the gold ring he stole from a dead man. El Kirilí was watching when they wounded Urbina, and he heard the order given to cease fire.

Martínez Espinosa, born in Las Nieves and a cousin of Urbina's, tells what he saw in all its simple detail: "Tomás Urbina Reyes had a crippled left wrist. With the first shots, they hit him in the right arm, totally shattering his forearm. He took another bullet in the ribs, and, unable to fire his rifle, he surrendered. His wounds weren't that serious, so he stayed inside the room until General Villa entered. Urbina greeted him with these words: 'I never expected this of you, *compadre*.'

"To which Villa answered, verbatim, 'Well, now you'll see the consequences.'" (Prior to this, Urbina's mother, Doña Refugio, and General Villa had been devoted friends, so there was hope that nothing would happen despite certain agreements Urbina was said to have made with the Carranzistas.)

Once up on his feet, Urbina walked out of the house at Villa's side, and they went over to the corner. They stayed there talking and talking. Nobody heard a thing, nor did they find out what was said. That conversation between the wounded Urbina and Villa lasted more than two hours. When they left the corner, Villa was holding Urbina by the arm and they were laughing. You could see they were pleased.

Nobody expected what happened a minute later.

When the two *compadres* got to where Rodolfo Fierro was standing, Villa said to him, "I'm going. My *compadre* will stay to have his wounds treated."

To which Fierro answered, hopping mad, "That wasn't the agreement we made." And he turned his head instantly toward his cavalry who had just about formed a circle around the hacienda and were ready to shoot.

Villa followed Fierro's look and gestures and said quickly, "Well, my *compadre* needs medical treatment. So, take him away, but first tend to his wounds because my *compadre* isn't well." (Those who saw the scene say that if Villa had defended Urbina any further, both of them would have been killed because the troops were behind Fierro. Villa didn't have a single one of his men there, and Urbina only a few who were with him in the hacienda.)

After that, Rodolfo Fierro ordered General Urbina into an automobile along with someone referred to as the doctor. Fierro himself got into the car with them. There were only four of them: those three and the driver. When they got to Villa Ocampo, the car was surrounded by about sixty of Urbina's men—all on horseback and all of them armed—who asked him, "What's going on, General?"

Urbina replied, "Well, we were captured . . . But from now on I'm not taking a single step unless you escort me."

The car left with the escort and got as far as the Berrendo ridge, where, because of the road, the car was able to make turns and climb quickly, leaving the horsemen far behind. Once at the top, it halted for a moment, but no matter how hard the horsemen rode, they couldn't even see the dust of the car, because it bolted ahead toward Las Catarinas.

That's where the gravestones are, one reading:

TOMAS URBINA.

The Commanding Officer
• Ordered Them Executed •

It was ten o'clock at night on Segunda del Rayo and the noise of a crowd was approaching. First some isolated shadows, then a whole group passed by our door.

They were leading three prisoners. Through the moving legs of the horses, pockets of light outlined their bodies. Their silhouettes looked the saddest. They were silent and stooped over, perhaps not wanting to know anything. Step by step, the noise of the crowd became more distant, and a while later came the sound of rifle volleys. Those nighttime executions were familiar occurrences. Men came down from the mountains, saw the sun set, and never woke up the next morning. This time, it was Herlindo Rodríguez and two others. They had been companions of Guillermo Baca and friends of Abelardo Prieto. They died, and no one knew why they were killed by a squad of men from the garrison headquarters. The commanding officer was Maclovio Herrera.

The wife of one of the men who was shot came to Parral and had the bodies exhumed. She looked at them for a long time, then ordered coffins for all three of them, headstones for all three of them, and had the graves enclosed by an iron gate.

The graveyard keeper, Juanito Amparán, said those gentlemen had been fortunate.

Perfecto Olivas, called El Guachi, left Parral for Santa Bárbara. Adán Galindo headed the squad of men. They all took seats on the train, and by chance El Guachi found himself sitting right next to Captain Galindo. People generally talk to each other on trains, telling each other private things as if they were old friends. These two said nothing until the exact moment they had to speak. Adán Galindo, the captain, spoke first. His voice intoned these words, "Listen, Guachi, if you're such a good shot, why don't you try hitting that old man over there?" He pointed out a man who at that moment was sitting on a trash bin. Olivas' only answer was to raise his rifle to his shoulder and fire it over the noise of the train. As always, his bullet found its mark.

From Santa Bárbara, Luis Herrera spoke by phone to his brother Maclovio, telling him he was going to send Perfecto Olivas back under prison guard so he could be harshly sentenced for his many serious crimes.

He was executed one cold afternoon, the kind of afternoon that makes the poor think of their helplessness. A timely blanket of shots put him to sleep forever atop his gray sarape with green eagles.

The execution began with the arrival of the troops who took their position facing the cemetery. Then, with slow and measured steps, the prisoner appeared. He was dressed in gray with his hat pulled down to his eyes, and he was smoking. A disgusted expression on his face showed clearly what he thought of the proceedings.

Maclovio Herrera rode up astride a spirited horse, followed by his entire staff. He stopped in front of all the people, choosing the place where he would best be seen and heard. Then, as the horse pranced from side to side, he shouted, "This man is a baaaandit! He's being shot as a muuuurderer! He killed an old man and kidnapped a young girl." El Guachi raised his hand in an effort to say something, but they paid no attention to him. He insisted, to no avail. Then he cried out, "A man who's going to die has a right to speak!" But they wouldn't let him. He flung the butt of his *macuchi* cigarette to one side and it landed by the fence. He spread out his sarape, pushed up his hat and uncovered his forehead, looking as though he were going to have his picture taken—the lenses of the rifles dissolved his pose. He fell heavily onto his gray sarape with green eagles. The troops marched off, and everyone turned their backs on the gray form left lying there, pressing into the ground the words they never let him say.

The smoldering butt lay by the fence. "Poor fellow," said Mama, "they didn't even let him finish his cigarette."

Maclovio, accompanied by his staff, went back to town by way of Segunda del Rayo Street. The dead man's tearful wife clutched in her fingers the last centavos he had given her. Felipa Madriles said that "she was going to eat them like bread with her children."

Martín López had a collection of snapshots. Wherever he went, he would stop to kiss them, and then he'd start to cry and get drunk. Martín López was a Villista general with blue eyes and a skinny body. Whether he was in a cantina, walking down the middle of the street, or stopping in doorways, he always had the pictures in his hand. Numbed with pain, he would recite their story, studded with bullets. "My brother, here is my brother, look at him, señora, this is my brother, Pablo López. They just shot him in Chihuahua. And here he is when he came out of the penitentiary, with one leg bandaged because he was wounded in Columbus." He showed the first snapshot, his skinny hand and blue eyes trembling. "Here he is facing the firing squad with a cigarette in his mouth. See him there, señora? Looks like his crutches are going to break any minute. You know what they say: *a dirty bullet is as big a pain as the gringos*. Well, if my brother Pablito hadn't been wounded, they never would have caught him." And, his eyes welling with tears and his nose running, he wiped his face with the grimy sleeve of his buttonless green jacket. Then he continued showing his inheritance, as he called it. "Here you see him with a cigarette in his hand, talking to the troops. My brother was a real man. Can't you see how he's laughing? I have to die like him. He taught me how Villistas should die. In this one, he's about to be shot. See how many people came to see him die? Look, señora, look, here he is dead! When will I have the chance to die like him?" he said, banging his head against the walls. "My brother died like a man, without selling out on his buddies hiding in the mountains. Viva Pablo López!" And he went on, as if sharing a confidence, "Do you know what he did? Well, he asked for breakfast. Oh boy, Pablito!" he exclaimed, laughing like a child. "You know something else? Well, he told them to take away a gringo who was in the crowd. He said he didn't want to die in front of a dog. Pablo López!" Martín shouted, as he went up the street, stumbling along on feet numbed by alcohol. "Pablo López! Pablo López!"

One rather cloudy afternoon Mama told me the Carranzistas were coming. Almost all the Villistas had evacuated the plaza when, from around the corner, a rider appeared with his body bent over his horse. Very slowly, he went down the street in the direction of the De Jesús Barracks. I saw him as he passed by the house. His eyes looked like two pools of dirty water. He wasn't ugly. He just had the face of a man lulled by fate. Half falling off his horse, he disappeared at the end of the street. Mama said, "Martín López, don't get taken prisoner. Your mother's blessings will watch over you."

III
UNDER FIRE

He said he had never felt as helpless as he did in León de los Aldamas. A local woman pointed out the road to him. He told us the townspeople used to show them the safest escape routes, and many saved their lives.

He hadn't seen El Peet since the fighting started at Celaya. Cheché Barrón had told him that El Peet had been hit by two bullets; his knees buckled under him from the one in his back that was pretty bad. "There's no way you'll find your brother," Barrón said to him.

El Ratoncito, an adorable horse, was with him. He was a very bad boy and very spoiled. He felt no sadness when he heard about El Peet's wounds, but when he was alone, that night in León, he did think of Mama and our house. He said he didn't cry. He probably didn't. He was bad, but El Ratoncito had light in his eyes and was a good companion.

El Peet was always the better one. He had no parents and was actually El Siete's cousin. He was seventeen years old when he went to fight at Celaya, and he only did it to watch out for El Siete. He wasn't a soldier, and didn't want to become one. This was his only battle, and he came out of it wounded. Chuckling to himself, the boy known as El Siete told Mama that, when he found himself all alone, he believed in God. Out in the wilderness, among some trees, he sat down to think. He was so tired he fell asleep without realizing it, holding his horse's reins by one hand. He said that just as he was dreaming that El Ratoncito had wings and they were flying together, he heard a shout that was Villa's voice saying, "Get up, son." He heard it so clearly that he opened his eyes just as Villa again said to him, "Wake up, son. Where's your horse?" Laughing, Villa and the men who were with him saw the lad quickly jump up and hold out his right hand, showing them his horse. El Siete will never forget it. It was the one happy moment of his life because he heard the voice of General Villa. "God rewarded me," he said, closing his eyes. "I heard Papa Pancho."

On the slope of La Cruz Hill, near Peña Pobre, is the house of Emilio Arroyo. Villa had turned it into a hospital. The wounded from the fighting in Torreón were brought there with their bellies, legs and arms shot through with bullets. In those days, Villa was master of Parral; he was always the master there. He had lots of wounded men and nobody wanted to care for them. Mama spoke with the nuns at the De Jesús Hospital and managed to get the most severely wounded tended to. Gradually, women and girls started arriving. There were many rooms full of the wounded, most of them lying on cots brought from the hotels in Torreón.

Mama told me to hold the tray for her as she made her rounds. First there was a thigh with an infected wound. When she squeezed it, rivers of pus flowed out. The man trembled and his forehead was sweating. Mama said she wouldn't stop until blood came out. When it did, she moistened cotton in a jar and placed it on the wound which she bandaged. Then came a head, a jawbone, about six more legs, a stocky man who talked a lot and had a bullet in his side, the serious stomach wound of an ex-general who kept his eyes closed, and another person shot in the buttocks. She treated fourteen in all, and I held the tray for her. Mama was very sympathetic toward those who suffered.

One day we heard the wounded men talking about Luis Herrera, "That dog got what was coming to him! He was sleeping in the Iberia Hotel in Torreón, and we came and wrapped him in a bed pad and threw him out the window like a sack. We laughed to see him hit the ground. Then we shot him right in the heart and hanged him. We pinned a picture of Carranza to his fly and stuck a fistful of Carranzista bills in his hand." One tall man with green eyes said, "If we had had something to take his picture with, we would have put it in a storefront for his relatives, who live here, to see." "That bum's face was twisted with fright, as if he'd seen the devil. He was really ugly!" they said, choking with laughter.

The news of the day was that Villa had given Baudelio a beating because he had executed some men the General didn't want killed. Each day there was something to talk about: "The Villistas are winning, so why are they staying in Parral and not moving on? Why can't they advance further?"

That afternoon everyone was whispering. Night was coming and people were moving out with the single thought that Pancho Murguía and the other Carranzistas were coming. By morning, the General had left. Only the foot soldiers, who always leave last, remained along with many wounded men. Very few could be taken along. The most severely wounded would stay.

Mama went in person to talk to the municipal president. She asked, begged, implored, and, if these words are not enough to get the idea across, I will say that she cried for the fate awaiting the wounded men. She went around herself, even paying people to help her save those men by transferring them to the De Jesús Hospital, where the nuns of Parral could care for them. The president told Mama that she was getting herself mixed up in trying to save bandits, but she said she didn't know who they were. "Right now, they aren't even men," Mama answered. Finally, they gave her some rolling carts on which the wounded could be carried to the hospital. In three hours the work was done. Mama came home very tired.

The Carranzistas arrived at around midday. Right away, they began to round up people. They took the wounded from the hospital, furious not to have found them in Emilio Arroyo's house. They couldn't be killed in front of the nuns just like that. They carried them to the station and piled them one on top of another into a freight car like the ones used for horses, paying no attention that some were gravely wounded. I was watching when one tall, blue-eyed officer climbed into the car and said, "The General's brother (I forgot the name he used) is among these men here." And then he kicked some of the men by the door, others he jabbed or moved to one side with his feet so he could walk among them, almost always scornfully. They said those men were bandits; we knew they were brave men from the North who couldn't move because they were too badly wounded. I was proud deep down inside because Mama had saved those men. When I watched them drink the water I brought them, I felt happy to be useful in some way. Mama asked the officer what they were going to do with those men. "We'll burn them with tar when we leave here, and then we'll blow up the car," he said to be offensive.

Mama had to go to the station. The Carranzistas wanted to know why she had taken the wounded to the hospital. As always, Mama answered, "They were wounded, some very seriously, and they needed care." She said that she didn't know anyone, not even the General. They knew she was lying, but they let her alone.

The wounded were dying from hunger and lack of medication. It was practically forbidden to give them water. Every night a group of men with a little lantern would go by the house carrying a dead man all the way down the street. Their lantern light swung in rhythm with their steps. Silence, grime and hunger. A wounded Villista, who passed by swaying in the light of a lantern that gradually dimmed and disappeared. The men who carried them there left them lying outside the cemetery.

Parral was under siege. Villa was defending the plaza. Sprinkled around the hills of town, his soldiers were resisting the attack. Rumors flew: "They kill. They plunder. They abduct women. They burn houses . . ." The town was helping Villa by sending cartons of bread, coffee, clothes, bandages, ammunition, pistols, and all types of rifles to the hills. The people were trying for dear life to avoid the bandits' arrival.

The attack became heavy near the cemetery on the Mesa and Blanco hills. They were coming from the valley of Allende, a town they had left in ruins. One afternoon some soldiers came down Segunda del Rayo Street; it was Villa and his boys. They were wearing yellow suits, and their faces were caked with dust. When they stopped in front of Don Vicente Zepeda's house, Carolina ran out carrying a rifle—the one she fired every sixteenth of September. She handed it to Villa, and he tipped his sombrero. The rifle hung from the pommel of his saddle as the group rode on.

By ten at night the gunfire was heavier. Flocks of Villistas ran by shouting, "Viva Villa!" Sometime later, the enemy entered town. It seemed as though the street was going to explode. They rode their horses along the sidewalks, shooting and shouting. The plundering began. Mama said that when she heard the rifle butts pounding on the doors, she shouted for them not to fire, that she was coming to open up. She told us she had felt very afraid. Some tall men entered, with three days' combat painted on their faces and rifles in their hands. In desperation, Mama ran to pick up little Gloria, who was three months old. When they saw her hugging her little girl, they took the child away from her, kissing and cuddling the baby. They were clearly delighted to see her. They said she looked like a little tuft of lace. Passing her from one to another on one hand, they kept kissing her. Little Gloria, all the while, kept her blue eyes open and didn't cry. Her little cap fell off, then her diapers, leaving her dressed only in a little vest, but she seemed happy as could be in the hands of those big men. Mama waited. One of them, named Chon Villescas, picked up a little blanket and put it around the baby. Then he handed her to Mama, and they left the house, saying good-bye very contentedly. Outside, they left word that others were not to disturb the house. And off they went, shouting "Death to Villa!" and firing their rifles into the sky.

No one knew how they apprehended him. Mama went to talk to the commanding officer and found him in a rage. A tall man with a ruddy, moon-shaped face, he was yelling at the top of his lungs, fire darting from his eyes. He strode back and forth, saying only, "Shoot them right now! Shoot them right now!" And he signed the order.

He was ordering the death of many, many, many, a great many men. Mama was so terrified that she ran straight to the station to talk to Catarino. In those days the troops had made the Parral station the center of their activities. That was where most of the people were, and it was like a beehive. Mama searched for Catarino's car, running as fast as she was able. "Mother of Mercy, take care of my son," she said, her forehead wet with perspiration. "Can you tell me where Catarino Acosta's car is?" she anxiously asked a man who had stars on his hat. Saying nothing, he pointed to some cars waiting in line. Mama broke into a run, but the cars had already moved. Then some other men said it was among the cars about to leave. "I'll go to the main barracks," she said, talking to herself, "because they're going to execute my son. Mother of Mercy, my son!" She ran in the direction of the waiting room, which was the way out. There were so many people on horseback, all with weapons in their hands. I ran behind her, and sometimes I was able to trot by her side. She never once took my hand. At times, I managed to grab on to her skirt, but, in her nervousness, she pushed my hand away, as if I were slowing her down, and she didn't even turn and look at me. When we got to the yard in front of the station and tried to cross, a tall man with long chaps was striding up and down, shouting a lot, addressing himself to another man on horseback who looked like a general surrounded by his staff. The one with the chaps was very angry, and he also had at his side many men with rifles in their hands, listening to what he was saying. I don't remember his words exactly, but all of a sudden the men on horseback drew their pistols and then put them away, as if to admit: we couldn't beat you to the trigger. The ones on foot then lowered their rifles to the ground. I've never been able to forget the sound of the rifles as they made ready to fire, the quickness and fearsome faces of the determined men on foot, or the expression of those on horseback trying to shoot first.

Mama was already talking to the commanding officer. "A telegram to the General, can I send it right away?" "How do you know where Villa is?" he replied. "No one knows that, not even us and we're Villistas!" Mama wasn't crying nor had she asked why they were holding my brother. "Your son knows where Perfecto Ruacho is, and we need to find Perfecto Ruacho. Your son helped him escape. Yes, madam, and showed him the road to Las Animas." Mama asked to see her boy, and she sat down to talk with him next to some dirty canvas covers that looked like a mountain of filth. That's where she began to talk to him, and each time a squad of men led a group out to be executed, Mama hid her son under the canvas and sat there without moving, making an effort to hold back her tears. The place was a frenzy of activity, men coming and going, shouting, working, arguing, and always the same words: "Shoot them! Shoot them! . . ."

While Mama sat there next to the canvas, we saw many groups of men led outside. Just then, El Chapo Marcelino came in, and he was shocked to find Mama there. He shouted questions to us over the din, then went directly to the officer in charge and came back with a paper in his hand, showing it to Mama, saying, "It's all arranged, I'll deliver it myself." At that, Mama put one hand to her eyes, reached for me with the other, and left, dragging me along. I didn't know what was happening, but I didn't take my eyes off El Chapo and my brother. When we were in the street, Mama wiped her eyes and said to me very gently, "Now your brother will not be killed. Let's go to church." And we went into Our Lady of Solitude, a church in San Juan de Dios.

We were walking along Mercaderes Street, almost in front of the Sonora News, when we heard a squad of marching soldiers. Mama stopped to see who they were leading away. "Four, eight, and four more is twelve," said Mama very upset. "Twenty-eight. How is it possible? Poor boys!" "Look!" I squealed excitedly. "There's the man with the long chaps, the one from the station, leading the way!" And I pointed my finger in his direction. "Yes, child, yes," said Mama, trying to soothe my young nerves. "I suspected they were going to kill them," she said, talking to herself as she stood on the sidewalk. "They're all from Durango, the ones who are dying, all our *paisanos*." She didn't want to walk along the same streets her countrymen were being taken, so we turned at San Nicolás bridge and went by way of De Jesús Hospital.

When we got home, El Chapo Marcelino had already been there and taken some blankets and pillows for my brother. Mama drank some coffee with brandy and rushed off to the jail. She said she hardly slept that night. The next morning she went to the jail again. "I was afraid I wouldn't be able to find him," she said with tears in her eyes. Two days later, she wrapped up some money and a holy medal and went to see her son off.

She returned alone. He came back once. He came to Mexico City, with the same look as when he left, exactly the same expression. He never said anything about Mama. He just began to flip a deck of cards he carried in his hand. The seven of spades, the seven of diamonds, his obsession. Now, where is he?

"We became Carranzistas this morning," said Manuel. El Siete asked him why, then, did the people still shout "Viva Villa" when they came into town along San Francisco Street. "I don't know," replied Captain Gándara.

The young soldier arrived at noon, looking more reckless than ever, with the face of somebody beginning to turn nasty and evil. Just come from Chihuahua and only in Parral for a few hours, Manuel was put up in a light-filled room. El Siete, with his broad, calm face and fearless smile, which later turned cold, took another room. He calmly lifted up his jacket and said, "Look at what we've got for you all in the mountains!" His body was wrapped in cartridge belts. He was feeling aggressive. They ate together. El Siete was testing Manuel's reaction; he never took the cartridge belts off for a moment. He was also wearing a pistol long enough to reach his knees. It was a gift, he said, from José Rodríguez. "You see, he found it amusing the other day when the flag was grabbed from my hands two times. I was going to reach for it again, but Papa Pancho wouldn't let me." He spoke brazenly to Manuel, trying to embed his words in the other's chest, as if they were bullets. Manuel, meanwhile, was playing with a piece of paper (he always used to make little paper boats after eating). "We have tons of ammunition, rivers of cartridges to wipe you out with," said El Siete, still wearing his hat and keeping his hand by his pistol. He was clearly eager to do Manuel in. But just then, a tan-faced man rode up in front of where they were sitting and stopped. He didn't say a word. El Siete went over to his horse, already saddled. As he was leaving he said something to Manuel like, "We'll be seeing each other sooner or later." Manuel changed into civilian clothes. "When that fellow comes back, give him my rifle and pistol," he said from the doorway, glancing down at the paper boat, fallen under the table.

In war, the young do not forgive. They shoot to kill, and almost always hit their target. Manuel surrendered without protest. His paper boat fell down too.

Samuel's Cigarette

Samuel Tamayo was very bashful in front of people. When he spoke, he would blush, lower his eyes and look down at his hands and feet. He didn't speak. He wouldn't even eat in front of anyone. Betita says he always went into the kitchen to eat. General Villa couldn't cure him of his bashfulness. "He's not like that with the men," said the General to Betita. "If you could only see him, my child. He fights like a true soldier. I really love Samuel. When we were going through the mountains, crossing Mapimí, dying of hunger and thirst, this boy—as shy as you see him now, my child—came and gave me pieces of hard tortilla that he had saved for me in his saddlebags. He took care of me as if I were his father. I love Samuel a great deal. That's why I'm entrusting him to you."

One day that timid boy, Samuel, went to sleep in an automobile along with Villa and Trillo. Went to sleep forever, struck by bullets.* Samuel was riding in the back seat and didn't even change his position. His rifle between his legs and a cigarette in his hand, he only turned his head to the side.

I think he was very pleased to die; now he wouldn't be ashamed again. He wouldn't suffer anymore in front of people. He embraced the bullets and held on to them. That's what he would have done with a sweetheart. The cigarette kept on burning between his fingers drained of life.

---

*Villa and his bodyguards were shot to death on 20 July 1923, shortly after driving into Parral, near where he lived. Villa had agreed to lay down arms after Carranza's defeat in 1920. (Trans.)

"José Borrego came from the district of Indé. Over by Cerro Gordo. What a man! How brave he was!" exclaims Salvador Barreno, sure of his words.

"In my long life as a soldier among Villistas, where I've seen many true and valiant men, I've never seen his match. José Borrego knew how to fight all by himself. Oh, he was really terrific! He taught many others the tricks of war between men on horseback and men on foot. He'd say to us, "Keep your head down, boys. Don't jump around, just aim for the other guy's head. Those are the best bullets. Don't fall asleep or get tired. Where there's a will, there's a way. One man can always fight against many, but remember, the secret is to fire at their heads.

"Didn't you see how I was trapped in the caves fighting against El Cagarruta and his men? Did they get me? Why not? Well, because I fire at their heads. And I keep my eyes on them until I see the dust of their retreat. I don't jump around when I'm hunting."

That mountain soldier got tired of giving advice. Salvador says that one day a bullet came—the kind that breaks down the best defense—and then José, that admired and beloved José, lay motionless, his eyes watching the dust, as he used to say, that, this time, covered his own face. But he couldn't see it.

The Virgin of El Rayo trembled with grief, and the stars almost fell off her robe. She shined so brightly at that moment that no one has ever forgotten it.

The way his companions tell it, Julio said to them, "I don't want to fight up there where you're looking. Not out of fear. I'm not afraid. It's the war between us that makes me sad. For the love of God, I'd rather be little again!" he exclaimed, laughing. Julio Reyes was always laughing. He was a young man, the color of wheat, and his coffee-colored eyes were kind, like those of a good man. When he passed by, he would talk with Mama. In Parral everyone knew each other and liked to talk. "Julio," Mama said to him, "here come the Villistas! Run! Run!"

The men who were up in the church of El Rayo had already taken defensive positions as they waited for the enemy. The enemies were their cousins, their brothers, and friends. Some shouted long live one general, and others cried long live his opponent. That's why they were enemies and killing one another.

Julio believed in the Virgin of El Rayo, and that's why she answered his wish. "I'd rather be little again," he had said.

They went down to buy cigarettes and bread, and Julio went with them. His tousled blond curls probably made him look more like a child who plays on the ground in the noonday sun.

The fighting was heavy. They had to crouch down at the corners, then dart across like papers carried by the wind. When they got back to the church, they all rushed in. Julio was the last one. Wounded, he could barely make it. He fell inside the doorway. When they went looking for him later, the miracle had been accomplished. Julio had become little, his body burned and shriveled. Now he really was a child again.

He had asked this of the Virgin, and she sent him a star from her robe. The star burned him.

They buried him in a tiny little box. The men who carried him to the cemetery rocked him with the rhythm of their steps.

The Watermelons

Mama said that the sun began to burn early that day. She was headed for Juárez. The suns in the north are strong, say the brown, weather-beaten faces of its men. A column of riders was advancing across those plains. Between Chihuahua and Juárez there was no water. Thirsty, they traveled closer and closer to the railroad tracks. The train going from Mexico City to Juárez takes on watermelons in Santa Rosalía. General Villa knew this and had told his men about it. They were going to stop the train; they were thirsty and they needed the watermelons. So they rode up to the tracks and, to the cry of "Viva Villa!" they stopped the convoy. Villa shouted to his boys, "Unload every last watermelon, and then let the train go on!" All the passengers were surprised to find out that those men wanted nothing else.

The march continued, and I think the tail end of the train, swaying gently, became a speck in the desert. The Villistas must have been very pleased. Each one was hugging his watermelon.

Right there on Segunda Street, Severo told me, between laughs, his tragedy: "Well, Nellie, now you'll hear how, on account of General Villa, I learned how to bake bread. Some other fellows and I were talking in the doorway of a house belonging to one of them. Only a few minutes before, the firing had stopped. The Villistas were in the plaza. Suddenly, we saw a man on horseback stop in front of the door. Then he hailed us saying, "How's it going, boys? This your bakery?" We returned his greeting and recognized the voice. Opening the door a bit wider, a ray of light fell on his face and we saw that it was indeed General Villa himself. He was the only one out there on all of Ojito Street. Although we knew it wasn't a bakery any longer, we couldn't bring ourselves to say so. We didn't dare; in those days, everything was suspect. Only the sign made it a bakery. The other boys were musicians, like me, and tailors. Very happily, we answered yes, and how could we help him?

"What do you need to make me a little bread for my boys?"

"Flour and sugar, General."

"Then I'll have it sent to you," he said, disappearing at a gallop. We were on the spot.

"Now what do we do?" we asked each other, pacing back and forth. "What do we do? Let's call Chema, since maybe he knows how to make bread, and between the lot of us, however we can, we'll make bread for the General!" I said to them, dying of laughter and fear.

Sure enough, they brought the flour and sugar, and Chema came on the run. We lit the abandoned ovens, rolled up our sleeves, and there we were, turned into bakers!

Out came the first loaves. We'd made them about a half kilo each. We packed them in some sacks, and I said, "All right, go to the barracks and take them to the General to see if he likes how they're coming out."

They say that when the General saw the sacks, he was very pleased and grabbed a loaf, sniffed it, and, laughing, stuck it in the opening of his chaps, saying, "What good loaves of bread! Keep making them that way."

The General never found out that we weren't bakers, and we all were glad to have been of some service to him.

Metallic and far ranging. His shouts, loud, clear, sometimes one after the other and vibrating. You could hear his voice from a great distance. His lungs seemed made of steel. Severo told me about it:

It happened in San Alberto, very near Parral. Severo had left Parral during a period of combat to pay a visit to his girlfriend, but being a civilian, he ran the risk of being taken for a spy. This was on his mind as he headed toward San Alberto, where General Villa also happened to be, accompanied by about five hundred men. When Severo got to his girlfriend's house, her family told him that, to avoid suspicion, he should start splitting wood in the patio. But Villa himself recognized that the young man was not from that town. After watching him for a time, he slowly walked up to him and said, "Hey, son, what's the latest news from Parral? You've just gotten here, haven't you?" Severo, quite surprised, answered quickly, "Yes, General, I've just come from Parral where the Villistas were fighting in the trenches. I got out as best I could, but it wasn't easy, because the firing was very heavy and the boys were in a bad way."

Villa's soldiers in San Alberto were under orders by the general not to approach the doors of the houses under any conditions, not even to ask for water. Almost all of them were camped around a field near town. They had already lit their fires and begun roasting meat for dinner.

When Villa heard what Severo said, he immediately let out a shout to his men. One of those shouts he would use in battle—vibrant, clear and moving, "We must go to the aid of our boys! The *changos* have pinned them down, and they need us! Let's go!"

Severo said that when all those men heard the General's voice, they stood up as one, leaving everything behind, without even touching the food. They ran straight to their horses, and before you could blink an eye, they rode off in a cloud of dust.

"The Villistas were one single man. Villa's voice could unite them all. One shout from him was enough to mount his cavalry." That's what Severo said, with the echo of the General's voice still ringing in his ears.

It happened in the De Jesús Barracks on the first street of El Rayo. My uncle saw it and told Mama about it. He tells the story at the drop of a hat. "All the men of the town of Pilar de Conchos had been rounded up. They had come to Parral to hide. The *concheños* were frightened and looked at each other as if kissing their lives good-bye. They were lined up in the entryway of the barracks. Villa came in, faced them, and said, 'What has Pancho Villa done to the *concheños* to make you run away from him? Why do you try to keep him away? Why do you make war on him when he has never attacked you? What is it you fear from him? Here is Pancho Villa! Accuse me! Go ahead, don't worry. I consider you *concheños* men, real men.'"

No one dared speak. "Talk up, fellows, speak," Villa said to them. One of them said he had been told that the General was very different now, not like he used to be. That he had changed toward them. Villa answered, "Men of Conchos, you have no reason to fear Villa. You have never done anything to me, so I will give you this opportunity: go back to your lands and work them in peace. You are men who cultivate the land, and I respect you. I've never done anything to Conchos because I know that people work hard there. Go on home, and don't fire on Villa again or be afraid of him, no matter what you hear about him. Pancho Villa respects the *concheños* because they are men and because they work the land."

Everyone was confounded, since they didn't expect those words. Villa had tears in his eyes, and he walked out pulling his hat down to hide them. The *concheños* could only look at each other in amazement. I know my uncle was surprised too, and that's why he'll never forget the General's words, and neither will he forget his tears.

Pepita Chacón, laughing amiably, recounted the time General Villa himself turned up at her house, just when a group of young men were dining there. They were the town dandies, their legs crossed under the table must have swayed rhythmically while their ample bellies surrendered to digestive horrors. No one knew when or how the General appeared before them. When they first saw him, he was already there. "Evening, buddies," he said smiling and coming closer. "Eating, eh?, well what d'ya know! A whole lot of your blood brothers wouldn't mind having a simple tortilla, and here you are drinking wine and smoking your fine little cigarettes." They say no one answered him, and some turned very, very pale. They sat there like statues, thinking that a single movement might cost them their lives. The General looked around for a chair and sat down. Then he tilted it back until it rested against the wall.

"I wonder how many of you will have to die?" he said, fixing his gaze on all of them as he felt around in his clothes for something. Finally, he took out a *macuchi* cigarette which he rolled with his fingers. "Just think," he said without looking at them, "when that no good Huerta had me locked up in Mexico City,* I taught myself how to smoke. I wasn't given to vices, but now I like my cigarettes." And he nonchalantly kept on rolling it around and around in his fingers. Suddenly, he looked at them, one by one, and said, "I wonder how many of you have fired shots at my boys? Because I know all of you have been in the Social Defense." Slowly, he looked down at his cigarette.

Up to that moment, none of the dandies, the *curritos,* as he liked to call them, had said one word. Raising his voice, he continued, "The Terrazas family didn't like me. They wanted to see me dead, but I won't die. Just the opposite, I get up early in the morning when my boys sound reveille, and I go around seeing how they are and what they need. I drink my cup of gruel and eat my tortillas. Me, die? Ha!" he exclaimed delightedly. And, as he lit his cigarette, his gaze turned to one of those men. Very slowly, he

---

*In March 1912 Villa was almost shot for insubordination while serving as an officer under Huerta's command, before the fall of Madero. Imprisoned instead, he escaped late in December of that year and took refuge in the U.S. until March 1913, a month after Madero's assassination. (Trans.)

said to him, "Listen, amigo, are you the one who showed me a hat in Guillermo Baca's store in Parral?" The fellow in question barely nodded his head to say yes. "Do you remember that your boss didn't want to show it to me? He didn't think I'd buy it. I lost that hat in a fight I had with some guys from La Acordada. Those damned *rurales* hated me as much as the *curros,* so as soon as they'd lay eyes on me, they'd start firing. When the day comes that my boys want to steal your sisters, then you'll really love the Villistas. But my boys don't like *curras,*" he said, getting up slowly and walking in the direction of the entryway. As he did, he smiled and said to them, "Well, now I've said hello, we've spoken, and we'll see each other again. Take care not to walk at night in the streets, because I won't be responsible." Then he told Pepita to turn off the lights to the hall and entryway so he could leave.

No sooner had he left than everyone came back to life.

"Man, what a scare he gave us," they said. "I thought he was looking for one of us," said someone. "I never would have believed it," another said. "Who would have thought he would suddenly turn up here?" And one after the other, the voices continued in their counterpoint. Then one of them asked, "Hey, what was that business about the hat? Tell us, what happened?" And the man he spoke to told the following story: "In the winter of 1904, he came into the store, just like many other farm people. He stopped in front of the counter and looked up at a hat that was hanging high above. After staring at it quite a while, he turned to Don Guillermo, who was busy typing behind the counter, and said to him, 'I want you to show me that hat.' Without moving, Don Guillermo replied, 'You haven't got the money to buy it,' and he kept on typing, paying no attention to him. The man thought for a moment and then said to him, 'Listen, I want to try that hat on for size.' I, being nearer to the hat, took it down for him and showed it to him. He tried it on and it looked fine on him, a perfect fit. Then he looked at me—I remember his eyes very well—and, handing over two pesos as down payment, told me to hold it for him. A few days later, he came back for it."

"What a good memory he must have to have recognized you!" said the elegant young men who had listened to the tale.

Those dandies, with big bellies and drooping cheeks, wouldn't forget the fright that man of war gave them.

"A hat shot off by the *rurales* is sometimes more interesting than the lives of some men," said Pepita to Mama, laughing at the elegant young men.

Isaías Alvarez said, "One time the General left some men as lookouts at a place in the foothills of the sierra while he went off to get money from Las Cuevas. When he returned, Don Carmen Delgado said, 'Let me go up first alone, my General, just in case something happens.' And so he went on ahead up to the house where the lookouts had been left waiting. Little by little, he brought his horse closer until he stopped in front of the door. The men, clearly disconcerted not to see Villa there, inquired of him: 'Where's the General?' Don Carmen replied, 'He's coming right behind.'"

Don Carmen later said he had noticed something strange about the fellows, and it suddenly occurred to him to say to them, "Will you bring me a pitcher of water?" One of them, who seemed to be the boss, and two others carried it out to him as if nothing were going on, but as he started to take a drink, one grabbed the reins of the horse and the others tried to pull him down. Quickly, Don Carmen lunged his horse at them, and just then shots were fired from inside the house, wounding Delgado and killing the two boys who had gone with him. Controlling his horse by hand, Don Carmen turned it around and rode off toward the desert, which lay in front of those who had tried to set up an ambush to kill the General. They kept firing at him, but since his horse was very good, he was able to ride it snakelike until he got out of sight. The two dead boys left behind were carrying some gold in their saddlebags. Don Carmen had about a hundred thousand pesos in dollar bills in his.

When he got back to where Villa was waiting, he told him what had happened. The General's only comment was, "How did you smell that out, Don Carmen?"

All Pablo Siañez's teeth were gold—Margarito Ortiz, whom they called El Chueco, had knocked his real ones out with a bullet—and he was executed in Torreón. When he was about to be shot, he asked someone to give him one last smoke. Then, with a hearty laugh, he faced the firing squad, saying, "I didn't want to die without puffing on a cigarette. We haven't had any for so long."

Pablito Siañez had been born in Cerro Gordo, Durango. Those who knew him say he was a very brave man. One day, at sunrise, General Villa himself executed him. Witnesses to the scene say that he tumbled from his horse, never to mount again. Why was he killed? They say he had a run-in with Villa, that they came to blows, that Pablo insulted the General, and in the exchange of words they took out their pistols. The fastest one—or he wouldn't have been the Jefe—was General Villa.

Pablo Mares died as he was spraying bullets from his cavalry rifle.

They say he was behind a large boulder one sunny day. His face was golden, his forehead well shaped, his eyes light colored, his nose straight and his hands broad. A handsome specimen. His children would have been grateful for their heritage. Even sickly and unattractive children—poor things—and their parents as well. In fact, both Pablos would have sired beautiful, robust children. I think Pablo Mares stopped spraying bullets from his rifle, and his strong body—the gift he gave to the Revolution—gradually keeled over on his left side; his hands slid down the boulder until they came to rest near the earth. His blue eyes didn't close. His rosy face died little by little. His broad shoulders lay at peace. All the blood running in bubbling red threads over the rock begged forgiveness for not having sired strong children.

Pablo Mares was one of ours, from our land. (He never dreamed I'd write this rhythmless verse to him.) I've seen his picture and I know his face by heart. He held me in his arms when I was very little. Mama said he sang me to sleep. "He was like a brother to me. He loved all my children as if they were his own," she said, holding the picture of Pablo Mares.

I think his arms fell asleep alongside his rifle after a song of bullets.

These men were resigned to their fate. No one—not even bullets—could stifle their joy of living. Neither the deceits of love nor death could keep them away from a street where they would congregate in the evenings.

"Listen, Gándara," said the pretty, smiling girls, "what about Rafael Galán—how did he die?"

And Gándara answered, "Well, without realizing it. That's the way Rafael was. He didn't realize it. He was a romantic, Rafael Gálan. We hadn't arrived at Santa Bárbara yet, where the fighting was, when he fell with a bullet in his forehead." And, by way of ending his story, he added, "He was so worn out, his heart no longer belonged to him. He had left it here on this street."

The young ladies seemed to grow a little sadder. "Poor dear Rafael," they said, looking at each other.

"He was not a poor thing! How could he be, if we gave him such a fine burial," said Gándara, and he began to tell exactly what happened to Captain Galán that day.

"When they caught sight of us, one of the enemy's advance parties sent us a bullet in greeting. Rafael, so nice and friendly, was the one who got it in the head and died right then and there on us."

"He was so handsome," sighed one blond-haired girl.

"Yes," said Captain Gándara, "so they say. That's why all the girls fell in love with him, and that's why we gave him such a lovely burial. We folded his arms, and his pale face, his little black mustache, his cropped beard, his dark brown hair, his nose—all of him looked even better than in life."

The young ladies cried, and Captain Gándara went on with his story: "We chose a field where there were lots of flowers, dug the grave, wrapped him in his blankets, and lowered him very carefully. Tears fell from our eyes when we shoveled dirt over him."

The girls were weeping now.

"Each one of his friends (there were a lot of us) put a bunch of flowers on his grave. Then we went on to Santa Bárbara, took the plaza, and more died. We left one of our garrisons there, and here we are back again. A really pretty death, Galán's," he said, ending his story.

"They killed Taralatas. His poor sweet mother!" said the girls. "But which one was he anyway? That tall, rather ruddy one who, whenever he got drunk, would almost make his horse talk to the ladies?"

"Yes, of course, he's the one. He would always go by shouting that shout of his: 'Hey, sweethearts, you don't scare me any more!' And off he'd ride."

They killed him here in Parral, over by El Aguila Barracks. El Taralatas—was that his name? No one remembers, but that's what they called him and that's how he died.

They killed Perico Rojas, Gómez, Chato Estrada. And they shot the Martínez boys. Sosita was lost in combat—the news passed that way from mouth to mouth. They all had favorite songs, which they left as an inheritance to others who loved them too. Those officers' songs brought joy to the street. They used to form circles on the corners, with their arms around each other's shoulders, to join voices. From there, each one would send out his song. Many young women were left single because these men died shouting in combat: Ernesto Curiel, José Díaz, El Pagaré, Rafael Galán, El Taralatas, El Kirilí, Perico Rojas, Chon Villezcas, and so many others. . .

There were lots of marriageable women on that street, where the young officers spent so much time. Loving glances, handkerchief signals, and all the language they could communicate.

Federico Rojas sang only one song, which he left to the poor:

When the poor man
is down and out,
not even his family
wants him around.
He's broke, a bum, a drunk,
working all day,
never enough pay.
Ah, what a black mark
poverty is! When the
rich man has his way,
everyone is pleased
to serve the señor.
For the rich man,
there's no jail, no punishment.
He does something wrong,
and never loses honor.
Ah, what a black mark
poverty is!
When the poor man woos the girls,
he's too broke, too aggressive,

too unfaithful.
For the rich man,
there's no jail, no punishment.
He does something wrong,
and never loses honor.
Ah, what a black mark
poverty is!
When the rich man woos the girls,
they all boast to each other:
the señor spoke to me.
And they say to him proudly:
Oh, Don So-and-So, my love is yours.
Ah, what a black mark
poverty is!

The girls of Segunda del Rayo forgot about the officers, and they bore
the children of other men.

This song belonged to all of them. They would sing it together, in a
circle, with their arms around each other's shoulders:

Ay, ay, ay,
what a party we're having.
As everyone will say:
they're honest-to-goodness Officers
just back from fighting.
Ay, Lieutenant, Captain,
sotol, brandy,
here comes the Captain.
Ay, ay, ay,
now the trumpet's sounding,
calling us to the barracks.
Here come the fellows,
here comes the Colonel.
And Kirilí, Perico, Rafael, Taralatas,
Federico, Federico.
Ay, ay, ay,
What foolish fellows,
we're going out to dance.
The *federales* are coming,
but they won't kill us.
Captain, here I am.
My pistol and my watch.
Lieutenant, ay, ay, ay.

No pistol shooting now,
'cause we're going to bed.
All Villa's boys'll be
ready to fight!

In the evenings their song keeps reverberating outside our doors, and they mingle with the shadows seeking the glow of moonlight. Their bodies get longer and look to me as though they want to be ghosts in the stories told to scared children.

Abelardo said to us:
I don't want to surrender,
but I'll turn myself in
to Hidalgo del Parral.

The soldiers' throats shouted out, rather than sang, these words.

Abelardo Prieto, a young man twenty years old, born in the mountains near Balleza, right in San Ignacio in the Olivos valley, had taken up arms with Guillermo Baca. It all began one November morning on La Cruz Hill. A handful of men, with the revolutionary cry and the tricolor flag, broke the silence of the town, firing shots through all the cracks where there were rural police. They seemed to be playing on horseback, riding across the plazas, up to the hills, shouting and laughing. Those who witnessed the uprising say it didn't look like one.

Don Guillermo Baca was the first revolutionary leader in the North. He protected the poor people of Parral, and they remember him with much affection. He was a merchant who knew all the mountain men, and he formed his troop with them.

On the night of 20 November they went up to the hill. The next day they came down firing and shouting "Vivas." Their standard bearer was shot during the charge. They all rode off toward the mountains where they fought at Sandías Mesa. Guillermo Baca disappeared. His horse turned up alone, its saddle stained with blood, but he was never found. Days and months passed. Nobody knew a thing. In Parral, the people cried.

They found Don Guillermo's bones in a cave. The people gathered in front of the Government Palace and held a wake for him. When they went to bury him, Abelardo Prieto shouted for all to hear that the Herreras were responsible for Baca's death. Then Abelardo headed for the mountains.

One day, the commanding officer ordered Abelardo arrested:

Circle round, boys,
come sing all together
the tragedy of Abelardo
as I shall tell it.
By order of the President,
the Captain and his men

must arrest and apprehend
Abelardo and his father.
Abelardo and his father
made ready to leave.
They said their farewells
to wife and family.
Abelardo said to us:
my heart is warning me
that this is the beginning
of a terrible betrayal.
To the Captain, Abelardo said:
I want to see your orders.
So they showed him the letter
which appeared authentic.
The letter said Abelardo
had nothing to fear,
he should surrender his weapons
and he wouldn't be punished.
His father said to him:
Son, we have nothing to fear.
We committed no crime,
so all will be well.

They were locked up in the Government Palace, under the threat of death. The Herreras did everything possible to finish Abelardo off. The soldiers from Balleza, captained by Cornelio Meraz, besieged the building. Each one held a rifle to his shoulder with one eye closed. Taking aim, they demanded that the prisoners be handed over. It all happened in a few minutes. The tragedy says:

The supporters of Prieto
gradually spread out
and proved their strength enough
to get him released.

Abelardo and his people left for the mountains. There, one night when father and son were unprotected, a man named Jesús Yáñez took them by surprise. In the little village of San Juan, upriver from Balleza, they were murdered by Yáñez and his squad of men. At the moment the shots rang out, Abelardo jumped into the river and died in the water by its shore, with the bullets in his back. They shot his father at the door of his own house.

Saturday, July the 15th,
how sad the plaza was!
That day they killed Abelardo
at the door of his house.
His mother cried with grief,
her heart broken in two:
now they've killed Abelardo
and my husband Francisco too.

Yáñez was a lieutenant in the Herrera brothers' gang.

Abelardo was only twenty-one when he died. He had been a Maderista since 1910. He began as the rebel leader of four men and ended up commanding a troop.

The barracks of La Sierra
were terrified to see
how Abelardo Prieto
knocked down the enemy.

Those who still remember Abelardo sing the tragic ballad. Such are the debts among men; they're paid with songs and bullets. The Herreras aren't singing. Their bodies shelter bullets that weren't meant for them. Nonetheless, Abelardo Prieto has been avenged.

The Green Leaves of Martín López

It was the fourth of September, but of what year? A cold bullet embedded itself in Martín López's abdomen. This happened after a battle in which the Villistas attacked the capital of Durango. López was shot at the hacienda called La Labor, and he died upon reaching Las Cruces. It was immediately known that Villa's second-in-command was dead. A few days later, Carranza's men arrived and disinterred his body. They wanted to see if it really was Martín López. They feared him so much that when they took him out of the ground, they stared at him, incredulous. They brushed off his face, cleaned his eyes, opened his shirt and saw where the bullet had lodged in his belly. They also lifted off some still green leaves that covered his wound. They did these and many other things to convince themselves that Martín was dead. Martín López, the man who had handed them so many defeats, that young general who wouldn't even let them sleep. They were very afraid of him.

General Villa wept for him more than anyone. He loved him like a son. Martín López had been his assistant since 1911, when he was only twelve years old.

Pablo, Martín, and Vicente López—three brothers—died being Villistas. The last one was Martín, who came to be the General's second and his son. No one had more right to call himself Villa's son. Martín even looked like Villa; he was his warrior son. Through him, the General accomplished his military objectives with mathematical precision. No one could have understood him better in the moments of battle. But that slim, blond fellow was erased by the earth his companions threw over his grave. His hands, agile at handling reins and dispensing bullets, were no more. His enemies might celebrate and his companions mourn, but another Martín López would not be seen again in these parts. (These were the words of a poet of the people who spontaneously narrated to me the death of General Martín López.)

Royal Dove of Durango, fly off to El Fortín, and tell the Carranzistas that here we buried Martín.

Martín López used to tell them, "No fear have I of you." And when it came to bullets, his aim was always true.

As his men attacked Columbus, Martín López was heard to say, "Let's burn down all the houses, and then be on our way."

At the hacienda La Labor, a bullet struck him down. Two days he lingered with us, and then his death came round.

"Men, don't ever surrender!" Martín López used to cry. "It's best to go down fighting; that's the only way to die."

On the plains of Catarinas, Martín made his pony run. And on the field of battle, they called him the devil's son.

He'd ride from here to there, shouting loud for all to hear, "I've got the *changos'* lightning bolt and quiver with me here!"

On horseback with his lariat, in Canutillo he lassoed them. Every one of them died there, not a single one left wounded.

In Chihuahua and Torreón, and in Parral so fair, Martín López led his troops in the art of brave warfare.

One day in downtown Chihuahua, astride his favorite horse, he rode up the steps of the building where the government maps its course.

He died in old Las Cruces, in the month of September, and was buried by Villa's *dorados,** as the people all remember.

Royal Dove of Durango, fly straight and in a hurry. Tell them that young Martín has just this day been buried.

Pancho Villa and his *dorados* have cried for the departed. And so have all the people, even the most hard-hearted.

All the hills of the North will remember our Martín. He rode up every one of them, by death 'til late unseen.

Fly ash-gray Dove, fly on, to that distant, smoke-filled place. Tell the Carranzistas: Martín rests in the mountains' embrace.

---

*The *dorados,* or Dorado cavalry, were Villa's most select troops and bodyguards. (Trans.)

It was February, and General Villa's troops had arrived. Chonita happily remembers it this way: "The wind was blowing and the brims of their hats were bent against their heads. Bathed in dust, mouths dry and eyes weary, they calmly surveyed the streets. They rode in on horseback, and they were happy to be there. The people who saw them still remember the way it was. 'Yes, of course, yes,' say the women. 'Over there came Nicolás Fernández, tall, slim, with highway dust all over his face. He went by here very quietly, and he stopped in front of the main barracks to talk with Villa. Then he turned his horse and left by way of that corner over there.' They extend a hand to point out the way and then go on remembering the faces and figures of those centaurs of the Chihuahua mountains.

"'Martín López, that boyish fellow, looked just like Saint Michael in combat. Don't you remember how the handkerchief around his neck would flutter as he bent over his horse and rode into the gunfire, right into the enemy ranks? Who could have stopped him? Bullets couldn't hit him. Martín, the one who cried when he remembered his brother Pablito, went off in that direction, through that alleyway,' and they point out a narrow little street full of stones. 'He was leaning forward over his horse. And from that other street, the enemy was riding into town. You could see his shadow as he jumped over battlements, but the enemy couldn't see him. Saint Michael was protecting him.' Voices repeat Martín's name—back where life has stopped and been preserved in the images of the revolution. 'Martín López, the brave boy, went that way.' And a gnarled hand, with broken nails and fingers worn by work, points toward the stone alleyway. 'He went that way,' say those women. 'He went alone with his soul, only looking at the hills, but when he heard gunfire, he'd laugh with us. Poor child, may God's peace be with him.'"

And Elías Acosta, the one with green eyes and black eyebrows, a beautiful man the color of a ripe peach, came along this way with his assistant. They stopped at Chonita's house to eat.

They had scarcely begun, when shouts came from the street: "The *changos* are coming across the bridge!"

"*Madrecita,*" said Elías Acosta, "I'll be right back. Make sure my soup doesn't get cold."

His assistant drew the attackers on while Elías Acosta fired on them from a hiding place in an alleyway. His aim was always true. Then they went back to Chonita's house to finish their soup and a cup of gruel.

Chonita brought them everything, running this way, flying that way. She knew it was the last time that man would grace the table of her inn.

"How much do I owe you?" he asked timidly. "We'll be going, little mother, because lots of *changos* are coming this way."

"Nothing, son, nothing. Go, and may God bless you."

"They rode off that way," she said, raising her dark and calloused arm. Chonita, the little mother of Elías Acosta and so many others.

The voices keep on asking:

"And what about Gándara? And El Chino Ortiz?"

"Yes," answer those women who were witnesses to the tragedies, "yes, of course, over there by that rock they knocked off his hat, and they killed him over there, in front of that house."

"Kirilí, Taralatas, each one tried to get away as best he could."

"They had come to town. It was February, and windy. Their eyes were weary and their hats were bent against their heads. Hands, whipped by the wind, cradled the reins of their horses. They only stayed a few hours, and then they left." The arms of those sometime *madrecitas* point out the places. "Poor dears, they didn't have time for anything. Will they come back in April? Or maybe in May? This time, one was left behind, and he still hasn't been picked up. The garbage cart will do it. We can't. If we did, the Carranzistas would kill us."

"But they'll be back in April or May!" say the voices of those good and ingenuous women of the North.

They reached Rosario and kept on going. General Villa found out and picked the most favorable place for the attack.

Martín López was charged with taking some cavalry troops and drawing the enemy. Ismael Maynez, a colonel on Villa's general staff, would go with Martín to attack the *changos* (Ismael lives in the Allende valley, in the state of Chihuahua). This was the order the Jefe gave us, says Maynez, "'Look, Martín, go and stir them up a bit. Don't waste much ammunition, but attack and then make like you've been beaten, right under their noses. Ride back this way to regroup, but take that path over there by those mesquite bushes, and wait there. The signal to attack will be the noise from these two ladies I have here' (and he showed them two hand grenades he had ready). He himself would throw them. Until that time, no one should move—no one, no matter what. 'Then, when the attack is under way,' he said, 'you, Martín, will take your boys and block that exit way' (and he pointed out a probable escape route). 'I want to trap them right here. Go ahead, Martín, move out quickly, boys.'

"General Villa had already spread out his men. Behind the hillocks on the slopes, they were all flat on their stomachs, waiting very calmly." (Ismael Maynez' blue eyes squint as if to capture the exact vision of his companions, lying there.) He keeps talking with the characteristic blankness of the men from the North when they are expounding their truths. "So we went off to find them. Martín, who was the spitting image of General Villa, used to do things so precisely that he never failed. He would carry out orders as if he were Villa himself. He had absorbed the General's every thought, and we could almost see that he was guessing what the General wanted. It made no difference if he was far away or nearby. Ah! That Martín was so tricky! How he could fool those damned *changos!* You had to see how he'd play with them. He'd do whatever he wanted," says Ismael, laughing heartily to himself, "and, when he and Elías Acosta would get together, heaven help my soul, what a pair they were! (We used to call Elías, 'the Shewolf'). Those two were incredibly mischievous and capable of anything. Unfortunately, Elías was killed very quickly. In every battle, we thought we'd lose Martín. Neither men nor bullets mattered to him. He'd take them on like the devil himself.

"We owe to Martín, under the Jefe's orders, some of the greatest defeats we handed to the Carranzistas.

"Following the orders he had, Martín López and his cavalry confronted the *changos*. They, in turn, approached with considerable wariness. The Villista cavalry, led by Martín López, didn't answer their fire. When we were almost face to face," says Ismael Maynez, "we hit them with a round of lead, and then we turned around without engaging in combat. Falling back little by little, shot by shot, we managed to get to the path the Jefe had shown us. Heading up behind the rocks, we dismounted and crouched down. The Carranzistas were coming closer and closer. They were already on the plains below. Still we heard nothing. The General hadn't thrown the grenades. Martín said, 'Take a look at what's going on.' So I climbed up into a mesquite and looked from there. The General was in the same spot, as were his men, and no one was moving. The enemy was practically on top of them, almost at the foot of the improvised trenches, and no signal had been given to us. 'I wonder what's the matter with the Jefe?' said Martín, anxiously, 'take a good look.' 'Yes, there they are,' I said, but without understanding what was going on. The fortifications were about to be breached. I climbed down quickly and gave Martín the glasses so he could see for himself what was happening. I still hadn't crouched down when the two ladies the General had in his hand exploded. Quickly, we mounted on the run and took cover to the side the General had indicated. My God, what an attack that was! Those *changos* were really frightened. That caused them to make a half turn. A mortal half turn. Martín's maneuvering was a pleasure to see. The Jefe facing them. Martín almost taking on the enemy's whole left flank. What a pretty picture that was! In the entire five years of our campaign against Carranza, we never again saw so many dead *changos* at one time. Two thousand eight hundred Carranzistas died. For Murguía, that ambush was one of his biggest failures. Even more so, if you take into account that at that time they considered us already defeated."

Ismael Maynez ends his story with a sip of coffee and looks up toward the Alto de la Cantera, where one day death would find him.

Mama said that the town of Parral had celebrated that victory and that one morning, after a snowfall, some dark, ragged shapes passed our street. A few were dragging rifles, others were on horses that could barely walk. They weren't so much human beings as shapes wrapped in grime, dirt, and dust—veritable apparitions.

My aunt Fela and Mama had seen them when they passed by Segunda del Rayo in pursuit of the Villistas. They were happy then. And today, had they dragged themselves all the way from Rosario? Mama's eyes had a lovely light in them. I think she was pleased. The people of our land had beaten the savages. Horses' hooves would be heard again.

Our street would be joyful once more, and Mama would take me by the hand to church, where the Virgin was waiting for her.

—·*My Mother's Hands*·—

··

By Nellie Campobello
Translated by Irene Matthews

Long before I translated her work, I had already met Nellie Campobello in Mexico. In 1981 she was still extremely feisty—physically, intellectually, and philosophically—and she regaled me one long sleepless night with memories and tales and songs and gossip. During some eighteen hours of "interview" she taught me how to dance her favorite folkloric steps, outlined her secret recipes (although she seemed to be living on fast food, chocolate candies—British were best—and brandy), introduced me to each of the twenty-eight cats who occupied two of the large upper rooms of her dilapidated house in the heart of Mexico City and to some of the many spirits with whom she communed in her rafters. She tattled scandalously in four or five languages about famous men she had known, and utterly refused to talk about her writing. Do words die when they get written down? Or did her published poetry, her prose, play such an infinitesimal part in her personal culture that they faded into oblivion in face of the more immediate stimuli of talk, and music, and dance, and, finally, breakfast at the local version of McDonald's?

I have been fortunate enough to meet Nellie Campobello on several occasions since then, in less happy and ebullient circumstances—her health has faded rapidly in the last few years. Despite her frailty, she generously gave of her time to talk about her childhood and her writing, but for perhaps other reasons now she seemed to be unable to clarify specific points I was stuck on in my translation; she "couldn't remember what she meant by that"—not totally surprising some forty years after the writing, and seventy years after the events themselves. More interesting, perhaps, was the selectivity of her memory, and the tone in which the eighty-or-so–year–old aristocrat still coyly evaded or embroidered or even parodied parts of her biography and her literature to sustain both a certain fantasy and a certain irony in her backward glance. The stories she told of her *mamá*, while still loving and admiring, had little in common with the lyrical eulogy that is *Las manos*.

In short, rather than illuminating occasional points of puzzlement in interpretation, the author's own commentary tended rather to complicate the whole question of tone: is *Las manos de Mamá* a thoroughly sentimental evocation or in fact a highly artistic and professional fiction? The one does not necessarily preclude the other, of course, and such conjecture may be completely irrelevant to enjoyment or comprehension of the final version, but such doubts persuaded me, as no other "authorial assistance" might have done, that Nellie Campobello's words and syntax should be translated as closely as possible to the original. Where there are obvious awkwardnesses or repetitions in the Spanish they are evidence not of some sort of poetical immaturity or ambivalence but of a specific, personal style that transforms biography and historiography into autobiography.

A few regionalisms and colloquialisms gave other problems, resolved in the main with the help of Campobello's contemporaries from the north of Mexico. Occasionally I reverted to informed guesswork: No one, not even Nellie, recognized her *barbas de ermitaño,* for example, but she on other occasions had talked about how her father made the children wooden toys, and how they loved to play with his tools and the left-over bits as much as they did the toys themselves. So the *barbas may* be the shavings that they stuck to their chins in moments of grand disguise. In a very few other instances I have incorporated into the text a word or two to imply a connotation in the Spanish that is absent in the English.

Las manos de Mamá is a poem, and poems are, perhaps, ultimately untranslatable. But Nellie Campobello really wanted to see her works in English, despite her role of the non-meddling authorial "muse." So I hope that my years in Mexico, my visits to Nellie and the friends who knew her and her mother and lived with her in her early and her later days, and my admiration for her writing have produced a version that is not too unworthy of the original. A number of generous readers in this country spotted errors and infelicities, polished off excessive Britishisms, and encouraged this publication. *My Mother's Hands* is dedicated to Nellie Campobello and her friends and mine who helped us reach a new audience.

The translation is based on the text of the second edition of *Las manos de Mamá* (Mexico City: Editorial Villa Ocampo, 1949).

• •

Mu-Bana-ci ra Mací Reyé
Busá Nará Mapu Be-Cabe
Jipi Cureko Neje Sináa.

• •

(A "Hai-kai" of the Tarahumara Indians: "Your face of light, mother, wakes and weeps, as before, today when I call out to you.")

Graceful as the mountain flowers when they dance swayed by the wind.

Her perfume permeates the air around the virgin madronas, far off where the light breaks wide open to the sky.

Her form can be seen as the sun sinks on the foothills of the mountain.

She was like the uncut wild cornflowers at the very instant they are kissed by the sun.

She was altogether a hymn, a sunrise. Her eyes reflected the corn sheaves as her busy hands crushed the golden spikes and made clusters that would become tortillas, dampened with tears.

Once I Sought Her, Far Away Where She Lived
——• A Life Shattered by Rifles' Ravages •——

I see the street narrower, shorter, sadder; gone are the shadows of its bodies and the rhythmic hoofbeats of the horses.

The earth is red, the sidewalks pockmarked, the lamps mere matchheads.

The people lean out of their doorways; they are the same; I don't need to close my eyes to picture it.

I am crawling on the ground, my hands are red, my face red, and the sun and my street—everything red like children's landscapes.

I was a little girl, and Mama was at the wicket gate calling me.

I am playing. Where are my friends? I run with the wind, wriggle and shout, open my mouth, swing my legs. I hear *Her* calling me, leaning over the wicket of the gray door: her black hair, her golden eyes—yellow and green in the morning, hazy at three in the afternoon; then, as if by magic, they would turn gold again. At that moment they were green, seen from the tramway rails; closer up, they danced with specks of hazel, yellow, and gray; her olive skin, her mouth traced with a slight curl on the left side. She shouted again, and again, to her daughter battling, wrapped in the earth, with her red landscapes . . . who came to *You* with the gesture of respect of someone facing her idol.

Her shout faded away so that I could see she was wearing a long dress, two spots of rouge, and there was no resemblance between this face and that other one, red from the sun. Besides, *You* were not at the wicket. If I had inquired, the good people of the Segunda del Rayo Street would have told me, "She went out, followed by her little children, she crossed the stone bridge to get to the train. She's gone . . . She won't come back again. But *She* is there, that's why you have come to look for her . . ."

And she was there, I saw her with my eyes, my own child's eyes. *You* made the miracle happen and I ran straight up to you. I was a child, *You* loved me that way. I leaned over the wicket. *She* is not there; the wood creaked and I, a woman now, dressed in white and without makeup, cried out over the door, "Mama, Mama, Mama!"

Reader, Fill Your Heart with
• My Respect: She Is Here •

She was born in the mountains. She grew up beside the wild berry trees, listening to fantastic tales. Her forefathers were warring men who had fought without truce against the barbarians to defend their lives and their plains. They would impale a redskin as easily as they would plant an arrow in the breasts of the wild beasts. From the watchtowers that protected their homes, they wielded their slings, their bows, to defend their lives.

Wild scenes passed before her eyes: "The barbarians had done, had, had . . . ," went the legend. How many of those people's scalps—beautiful long locks—had been torn out to adorn the belts of those Indians who were called savages? The valiant slings were stretched wide in the sunlight, the bows bent powerfully to spit forth light, deadly arrows. The war songs and dances, the heroic defenses, the pretty women, the bright bonfires—symbol of the life of these people—the feudal enmities; she was told all this and more. In her eyes exact visions were engraved, in that way her heart was forged; no one could belittle it, as no one can shatter the dawn.

The holly-oaks, the golden arbutus, created in the miracle of *Her* birth there. She was one of those women to whom everything yields as they pass by, not with virginal beauty and immaculate features: she was nature herself.

Her father: a tall man, his hair cut short above his collar, a wide cape, thong sandals on his feet and a keen steady gaze; in his youth some Comanche warriors had punctured his shoulder. He could knock a man down with a single swipe; he sold a house for a measure of coarse tobacco and a bottle of sotol. He slept sitting up in the middle of the patio. On awakening he would sing hymns of praise to give thanks to the dawn. He died one morning when the rifles and machine guns came to waken him. They say he said, "I am dying because I cannot fight."

"Blessed Jehovah, my rock, who trains my hands to battle and my fingers to war," he would stay in his man's songs, in the mornings perfumed with the scent of the wild shrubs.

"Oh! God, I will sing to you, I will sing you a new song with my psaltery, with music, I will sing to you. . ."

"Blessed are the people who have this:

"Blessed are the people whose God is Jehovah."

Papa's psalms.

"Papa Grande" they called him. Papa Grande, I say and will say.

I admire him because he carried within him the beauty of the mountains and because he simplified the mystery of life by singing to the dawn. I cannot imagine him with white shirtfront or black lapels, the adornment of men imprinted into family portraits. I love him, tree without flowers, with its great arms open wide, celebrating life. Under its shade I think of Papa Grande. He is there, the leaves sing of him, the wind shouts his name in my ears. I find myself in my grandfather: he loved the rivers and the great plains. He carried nature's panorama in his eyes and steered clear of the refinements of household reunions.

Oh, Papa, when I think of you, I feel close, very close to you. Every day your advice and words solve my petty problems. You knew the truth in every corner of your people's soul. The happiness in your eyes showed your kinship with the dawn, the rivers and the fields.

You never let anyone beat children. How you defended us when we hid under your cape and you, waving your stick in the air, would not let anyone touch us. Then you'd give us rose-colored peaches.

What defiance you showed in the face of oppression, and chagrin when someone did not obey the laws of nature! What approval when you saw your favorite daughter—*Her*—follow the dictates of her heart as though ordained. How many times you raised your voice in her defense. What would she be up to? Climbing a tree, riding a horse, singing, laughing, frolicking like a little wild fawn at playtime, always the same. *She* was allowed to do what she wanted, when she wanted, without pointless restrictions; the touch of nature in her own nature made her what she always was: a flower.

Papa, how I love you, and need your company so much. Wherever I go, your picture goes with me. I confide in your face, talk to you and ask your advice. You prayed directly to the sky and summoned God and Saint Michael, and I too speak with them and tell them in your own words how you want them to protect us. I know that you can hear me and I know that no one will ever dare harm us. I would like to tell you all this and a thousand other things, but the people who inhabit the world we live in fancy that it's madness to seek the smile of a dead Papa Grande. They prefer the smiles of unknown men and women, and not exactly smiles of spiritual comfort; no, they search for a smile that satisfies socialized, fictitious passions, which you avoided so hard.

Even so, Papa, don't forget to stay with us always and give us your blessing.

Love.
His eyes had not arrived.
Fifteen years invade her eyes and her body.
She does not know him.
He still did not appear.
Did she unknowingly steal the hearts of those who dared to believe themselves close to her life? Were those men ruined? Their lives shattered? Nature has always been innocent. So, are the mountains to blame for being tall and beautiful? And the water in the mountain streams? And the trees, and the flowers?

Tradition ruled that women did not marry strangers or outsiders.

Whenever she received letters and tributes from those who admired her and besieged her, she always gave them to her father and her brothers. She never lied to her family; she kept no secrets from them: they were her best friends.

Like the mountain streams, she was clean, whole, crystalline.

When he appeared, her hands reached out to touch his shoulders.

Our life flourished. She smiled at us as mothers do when they are part of their children.

She gave us her songs; her feet embroidered dance steps for us. She gave us all her beauty and her youth.

She was slender, lithe, agile; her clear, lively eyes engraved themselves in our hearts. She would gesture with her arms until they took on the precise outline of the mountains. But she was our mama, and her laughter was her gift to us. She played, ran about, she didn't seem like a grown woman; at times she was as childish as we were. To make us happy she blotted out the horrible anguish brought on by the last moments of our revolution. She would fly above her sorrows like the swallows heading for the place of no return, and always pushed her problems far aside. Us? Hunger? Flour tortillas, roast meat? We might as well close our eyes till the next day.

Mama: *You* were our artist; you knew how to erase sadness and hunger for bread from your children's lives forever—bread, which sometimes nobody had, but which we never needed. *You* managed to make us forget things that were nearly impossible for us.

Today, among the colored lights of the streets, wandering over the dirty tram rails, I stretch out my arm to *You*. It is dusk, as it was then, and I say to you:

"Mama, dance for me, sing, let me hear your voice. The bread in the shop windows does not exist. It's a lie that we need it. I want to worship the tips of your fingers. I want to see you embroider your eternal dance for me.

"Mama, turn your head. Smile as you did then, twirling in the wind like a red poppy shedding its petals."

Her children's hands stretched out to ask her for food.

There was war, there was hunger, and all the usual small-town stuff. We only had Mama. *She* only had our hungry mouths, with no understanding, no heart. Our reality was a round flour tortilla, a full cup of coffee.

She was alone; her companion lived in her memory. The strength of her love sustained her slender woman's body. There were tears in the bread she gave us.

She would get up early, go out: she walked a lot. What might *She* have been saying to herself, as she listened to her footsteps? What was there in her heart for him, who traveled with the rifle brigade? Dreams and hopes imprisoned her spirit! Tears fell daily from her golden eyes and dried in the wind. A long route; some bare streets, others slightly better; unwelcoming sidewalks, a stretch of open ground, an upward slope, and then that house of my aunt where papa left us and where we lived waiting only for *Her* return. We peered out from an entryway of slick blue flagstones, searching for the little black speck that, at a distance, formed her body. We would burst with bliss when we spotted her approaching: Mama was coming back, she was here, we came back to life. She did not cuddle us, didn't kiss us: with her hands she gathered us close to her heart.

She would come inside the house, let down her hair, sing, walk to and fro; almost without noticing, she would put us to one side. She moved things about here and there. She would light a cigarette and sometimes sit in the doorway looking at the patio and the old doors of that house on the outskirts of town, sad, so sad. She would look around her and become pensive; sometimes she twisted a ring she wore, puffed fiercely, fiercely, and almost closed her eyes. We wouldn't make a sound, then.

As it grew dark, she would seat us all around her and give us what her hands had cooked for us. She did not speak to us; she was simply there, quiet as a wounded dove, pure and gentle. She seemed like our prisoner—I know now that she was our captive. She would pick up her book and pray. She didn't tell us to pray. Later, from our bed, we could see the glow of her last cigarette: a star in her hands, it drew our eyes like a flour tortilla on hungry days.

She did not tell us fairy tales nor ghost stories; she told us about real happenings: Papa Grande, Saint Michael of Bocas, our land, the men of the Revolution, things about the war that she had seen with her own eyes. Those were her chats with her children. We were happy: we knew nothing about bogeymen. That was the way *She* wanted it.

Soldiers. Rifles. Bread. Sun. Moon. Her hands. Her eyes. The glow of her cigarette might be a tortilla between her fingers, but like our life, it was the light that clung to her fingers to absorb her own light, as we did, too.

The red hands of healthy children always seek contact with the earth.

The earth was our companion; we played with it in the sunlight. That earth—red like the palms of our hands and the heels of our feet—opened its arms to us and protected us until Mama returned.

With smooth pebbles and colored berries, we built little corrals of cows and bulls. They were our livestock, or so our inner world told us. Our minds could already live on the unreal. We had our treasures from childhood. We have them still, in jumbled cardboard boxes or in mirrored wardrobes. It doesn't matter where, they're our treasures.

The tribe playing with red earth, making mud pies, little corrals, houses, digging out the shiny berrystones. "This skinny speckled stone is a little heifer; these are bulls; we'll shut the cows in here; these are calves." Just like real life, and we shall not deceive ourselves; we will go on living in the unreal. When we close our eyes we can reach everything there. That's why we close our eyes.

Sequins and ears of corn are different. If rain falls from the sky onto sequins, they disintegrate. Grains of corn swell up and offer themselves to empty stomachs.

Everything comes to an end: tables, chairs, lace flounces, cakes, the color of healthy children's heels, tablecloths, cups of tea, rings, gold and silver coins, sacks of corn. When we are born we do not bring any of these lies with us. So, why suffer to obtain things that are lies? Why not just close our eyes and hold out our hands? Mama taught us that.

We know that *She* will laugh to see us still playing with the red earth: the heifers here, the bulls there; the cows in this corner, the mares running over here . . .

People who live off lies will say, "But those seeds are beans! We eat them in soup!" But since they don't exist in our world, we do not hear them. On the other hand, we see *Her* smile, telling us, "Yes, children; play; that's why you have your mother (that's how she'd speak to us, back then); and if you want to break the cups, go ahead and break them."

For *Her* a smile was worth more than any cup, an ear of corn more than a sequin.

The shadows of the street are elegant. The rails of the tramway are men's arms, open, not like a cross, but parallel to the poor hearts that skid over them.

Children's memories are fragmentary. I don't recall how or when we moved house. We were already living in another, where the tram rails were nailed to the ground in front of us, shining with long reflections like daggers and making a grimace that was a cruel smile if we looked down on it from the flat roof.

Mama said, "They're rails"; we said, "They're rails." They were supposed to be the tramway's, but the tram never came by.

Here everything was different. Mama no longer got up early, now she spent more time with us.

The sun did not shine straight down, somehow it seemed more elegant; there were more shadows. In the shade people did not wrinkle up their faces so hard to greet each other or to reply, or simply to speak the formal words that are not for children, and which we sometimes laughed at for their false tone—party talk, my little girl's voice called it—which people use to address one another when they are being grown up, men with beards and women with long dresses.

In our lives, this house marked those days that people call "unfortunate." For *Her*, such a thing did not exist; she did not complain. We knew nothing about poverty. Everything was natural in our world, in our game. Laughter, flour tortillas, milkless coffee, tumbles and broken heads, dead bodies, rifle volleys, the wounded, men rushing past on horseback, the soldiers' shouts, grimy flags, starless nights, moons or midday; everything was ours—everything—for that was our life. Mama's singing, her scoldings and her lovely face were ours too. We seemed like little old people, our eyes screwed up to discern life, light, cups, doors, bread. Our legs would tremble when we tried to climb up or down. *Her* skirt was our safeguard, our refuge. It could rain, thunder, lightning might flash, hurricanes blow; we were there, behind that gray door, protected by *Her*. Her slender figure, and the fall of the folds of her petticoat, imprinted our eyes with an unforgettable mama.

I see You *today as I did then; but the folds of your skirt move very fast and take you far, far away, where life does not reach and where* You *can no longer protect us from lightning bolts, nor from clouds of dust, nor from the water that scourges our eyes.*

One hand fine and white, the other sunburned and hard. They are two different hands, but they can be the same.

We knew nothing about life in the cities, not even from books, because we were children and couldn't read yet. We had all our familiar things there: Mama, the mountains, rivers, soldiers on their horses, flags dancing in their hands, and Mama lifting up her black hair to the sunlight.

It was possible to ignore the cities where people have the power to name each act of life; where there are shop windows full of lights, cakes, silk stockings worn by children who have shriveled lips and mothers with painted faces and organza outfits and reluctant smiles; where people walk faster and have no time to know each other, and suffer because they have no mirrors and colored windowpanes in their houses, and are happy only when they manage to look as though they have more than other people; where they believe in lighted salons and gilded plate and adore green sequins, but do not know that out there in the countryside bones and eyes grow stronger, and the cold burnishes bodies so they don't have that pallid flesh that looks like dead fish bellies or fetuses pickled in alcohol; there children do not live in the fetid atmosphere of at-home soirees where people smoke and drink and do not have healthy fresh breath.

We were grateful to *Her.* She kept us ignorant of the city just when we needed to be, and gave us the life our bones demanded.

Ignorant: the right, exact, perfect word.

In this house we learned the color of things and saw for the first time that Mama had two large moles and one small one; that her colors were natural; that she herself made everything we ate; that she washed our hair and made our little smocks (brothers and sisters were dressed the same; she would think up the patterns according to the pieces of cloth she had); that *She* did everything for us, with her own hands: for us little nobodies. They were happy little rags, made with the songs she sent out into the night in memory of her companion!

In our house there were flower pots, a portrait of Papa Grande, doves of all colors, two dogs—Zephyr and Nelly—a gray door with windows, the crossties and tracks of the tramway, a strip of sunshine that never disappeared from the street for a moment, and Mama's two hands, strong and healthy. The light in her eyes was our life. The eyes of a young woman, capable of finding her way in the dark without stars. For us she ransomed the happiness we owe her today.

Our life at that gray door grew more appealing every day. In the mornings, when it was cold, we would sit on our calf hides in the rays of the sun. We would laugh with the soldiers. Sometimes they'd sit down with us and we could understand them. "They were more like children and better"; they gave their lives with a smile and asked for nothing in return; we gave nothing and accepted everything.

The rhythm of drinking milk with sweet potato and our coffee and rolls was broken by a piece of news: "We no longer had a papa." Who came? I don't know, it's impossible to remember. What time was it when they took us away? Did we go by train? On the wind? Mama dismantled the machine she sewed our smocks on, wrapped up the main screws in a cloth, and put them away.

Now we were in Chihuahua. The house was pretty, but had no light nor air, which belonged to us because they were given to us by *Her* mountain.

The treasures had disappeared: even Pirala didn't bring a single one of his colored bobbins. There was a parlor, as posh people say, or rather a large room with a wooden floor, smelling bad, and old. There was a black folding screen with silver herons embroidered on it. How elegant that sounds! Our little beds, made with mama's songs, wrinkled with humbleness under the gaze of those imposing silver animals. The impression of the first moments faded in a few hours. In fact, what was the use of those big birds stretching out their beaks? We couldn't do anything with them. On the other hand, in another corner stood a wooden bench: on top it had nails, screws, little boxes, wheels from a lathe, and clumps of wood shavings—"hermits' beards." "Treasure!" our eyes told us, and we rushed at it, puffing out the wrinkles in our nightshirts.

Pirala divided things up. He was a mute, but he ruled over us. He kept the beards for himself. Our eyes got bloodshot with sadness: we wanted the beards. Our dictator asserted himself with his gaze, his sunburned face gleamed, he would tighten his mouth, lower his brows, clench all his jaw muscles and impose his will. We would be quiet. We couldn't live without him. We burst into action. When they put us into that big room, they said, "That's where you play." That is the word given by serious bearded persons to children's lives. They should have told us: "Live." Our problems were serious, huge, magnificent. Children's lives, if no one imprisons them, are an uninterrupted film.

"Here there is a fadeout," goes one scene. "Then a window appears, then a shoe." Sometimes life starts with a sandal and fades before a golden doorknocker. . . And Mama, where was she? We didn't see her at all. We wept asking to see her, and forgot her as we fell asleep.

Our experiments there in the big room, where we had the treasure bench and the black screen, our squabbles, our tears when we did not see Mama, that was our life. Food? I don't remember; it does not appear in any of my scenes. I don't think they gave us wheat tortillas.

One day *She* appeared. She was at the door of the big room, watching us. Her expressive face was vague: no smile, no tears, not a word. We did not cry out nor rush up to her: we simply came closer and closer and placed ourselves under the power of her skirt.

Then *She* said out loud, "I have come to take my children away." "No. No. No . . . ," angry voices replied. "Let's go, children," she cried, and walked away with the assurance of one who is not afraid and who knows there is no law that punishes for taking what belongs to oneself. We had taken several steps from the doorway of the big room into the patio. "You will not take them away!" said those voices. But nothing could deter that slender body that had given us life. Surrounding her, we allowed ourselves to be led off little by little until we saw the red earth of the street and were with her inside the car. Where were we going?

That's what our life was like. Where? How? Only the power of her skirt was real. *She,* the flower to which we clung like bees; we, the ones who drank everything from her and left her nothing.

I hadn't forgotten the night when a tall lady with a delicate nose took me by the hand without saying anything. Big doors being opened, the noise of bolts. Mama, there in a room lit by a dim bulb, seated on a small bench breastfeeding her little daughter. They greeted each other, *Her* face was sweet and calm; the beautiful lady's was sad and uncertain. I sat down on the floor, at Mama's feet, looking from one to the other. That figure, whom I did not know, talked standing up, walking about.

"Everything is ready for tomorrow," she said, in a very secretive way. "Who is she?" my curiosity asked. "There is no hope," she continued. "Everything is against you, have faith in God; those people are very strong and what they want is to take your children away from you."

"My children are mine," said her clear voice. "No one will take them away from me."

Their voices and their words led me to understand that *She* was in danger.

Were the laws of men trying to spoil our world?

The beautiful lady went out, leaving these words behind her: "Only God can save you. Have faith."

I went to sleep.

Now I am in a train going to Parral. *She* is there, serious, subdued, giving us little pieces of watermelon, with love.

Men's law is good as long as the weak have their place within it.

We appear in Parral. How much time has gone by? Everything seemed blurred to me. Did I live? Was it me? My life was a counterpane of colors, with no reason for being. It existed in the same way that the stars live for children's eyes.

That evening I saw her light a cigarette. She was telling a man with clear eyes and black brows everything that I hadn't managed to understand the night the beautiful lady spoke with her, when God appeared through Mama's hands.

"When my cousin went out," said Mama, "she left me thinking. God was my only salvation; I understood then that I held things in my own hands. I tore my blouse and a sleeve. I waited for the morning, and with my little daughter in my arms I came before my judges. I did not raise my eyes to look at them. I heard my enemies' voices. They were accusing me. Everyone was arguing. My eyes, my heart, my hands were knotted into the little bundle that my one-year-old child and I formed. I didn't move. Why should I? I held my defense in my hands. What was I going to say? I didn't know. I was only just recovering from the fright given me by all those strange words people in the city use. I realized that the law made by men was going to help me. I quickly thought of my father, of his advice: 'No, my darling; you have to stay inside the law to defend yourself. Those shyster lawyers and clerks are very technical people,' he had told me.

"Only God could save me? Now I understood. My faith was in Him; that is why I looked inside myself.

"'They are my children,' I said, with no wish to offend the distinguished atmosphere in the chamber.

"Again the voices shouted against me.

"The law spoke.

"'They are my children,' I told them once more, afraid of their shouts.

"The voices went on shouting and shouting.

"'My children, mine, of my flesh, my eyes, my soul, mine alone,' I repeated without raising my voice.

"The voices got louder. They were making me suffer.

"The law spoke.

"I remembered God, I turned my eyes on myself, I showed them my torn blouse and said, 'Look here; this is the proof.'

"The law spoke: 'This is the crime,' it said, pointing with a thick black hand at the tear in my blouse.

"The voices were no longer voices, they were relentless bellowings.

"My God spoke. 'That is a long tear, you can tell it was ripped with great force.'

"The law was represented by a dark face with ignoble features. It found the defense against those voices and said, 'There is no crime; you may withdraw, madam. Your children are yours.' I, to myself, said, 'I committed a crime in going for my children. The law? Yes, the law has served me well.' One lie pulled me under, another lie saved me."

"That is how the law works," *She* said to the man with the light eyes, drawing fiercely on her cigarette. "Sometimes it says that the children born of our own flesh are not ours, but a timely rip in a blouse confounds the eight hundred pages where it is laid down."

She shows a way: the only one.

"The general told me, 'I have to look out for them. They are fatherless because of the revolution.'

"'The father of my children,' I told him, 'my companion, went happily to war. He was defending his party and died doing so. We have lost him, no one can give him back to us. My children are mine and the favor I ask of you is that they be left with me. They do not need to be given anything on account of their father's death. Leave them with me.'"

She had explained all that, in a soft voice, to the man who smoked by her side, seated in the doorway of the house. "I want nothing for the death of my companion."

She steered our future. Her simple words, spoken with the modesty of that certain kind of woman, worked the miracle of not converting us into the wards of a revolutionary chief.

Where are *You*, my lady, so that I may worship your hand? Are you in the sky, where my eyes see you? Or perhaps your slender figure wanders, swayed by the wind, along that glorious street of the Segunda del Rayo?

Your words, transparent and humble, created our present freedom. We owe *You* everything, for no one, no one helped you with us. We belong to no one but *You*.

She formed us that way. No one who does not give us love can ever give us anything. We shall always be masters of our footsteps.

The Men Left Their Mutilated Bodies Awaiting
• the Succor of These Simple Flowers •

These people thought with their hearts. Judge them accordingly.

We saw the winter sun again: our own house, the tram rails, the elder tree, the doves, the portrait of Papa Grande.

Colonel Black Ear came to the house; he made his horse knock with its little hoof. *She* went out, and with scarcely a glance at him had guessed everything. The whole family was being destroyed by the revolution. "Who?" she asked in a still voice. Ruacho replied, "Arnulfo. Yes, at El Ebano." "And in Ojinaga," she said. Without dismounting, the colonel made his remarks in a certain tone, almost cynical. He seemed to be saying, with a smile, "We will all die, all of us, all of us. They were merely the first." Their ideals were demanding their lives. Cartucho told Mama, and so did Kirilí, "They were all going to die, all of them, every one."

"We are going to quarter the troops," said Ruacho, spurring on. "If nothing new happens, I'll come by later."

Life was like that: a bit of information and a man spurring his horse.

Not long afterward, bullets destroyed Colonel Black Ear. (Perfecto Ruacho had a mole on his ear.)

She dedicated herself with real love to helping the soldiers, no matter whose people they were.

"Why did you take in those men? Don't you know they are enemies?"

"They are not my enemies; they are my brothers."

"But they are savages. Do you protect rapists?"

"To me, they are not even men," she said, absolutely serene. "They are like children who needed me and I gave them my help. If you were in the same condition, I would be with you."

They would keep on trying to make her believe that those men were wild beasts. As if they were strangers! They were immaculate soldiers of the revolution. The bandits were the ones standing there, shouting at Mama, dressed in English style—in looted civilian clothing—and studded all over with silver links.

She always protected our boys, tall warriors with golden bodies.

How many things did she do on their behalf?

God knows. *She* and they know. Those who once were, are; those who do not know, never were, and never having been is like not being; because that is the nature of these affairs the soul transacts: not being when you should have been is not to be when there is no need to be.

It was the sixth of January, Epiphany. We knew nothing about the coming of the Three Kings, but that was the Three Kings' Day.

It was midday. A loud bang was heard, the whole street reverberated, the houses trembled. My little brother's arm, in shreds, appeared dragged by a blackened body; his face and clothes destroyed, black. He was encrusted all over with lead. He ran to bring his broken flesh to Mama. First they walked one block: they were going to get a doctor. Then they turned back, because they could no longer go on: the boy was dying. As if crazed, *She* ran to and fro. Her child was dying. She cried out to God, begged the Virgin, wept.

They took him to the hospital; we did not see him until one week later. Mama was constantly at his bedside; it was as if *She* had lost her arm.

There were nuns at the hospital, and they said that for them, my brother's muteness made him a little saint.

He wore a white gown like a smock and people always noticed him there in the lovely garden tended by the nuns in the hospital of the Sacred Heart of Jesus. He really did have the face of an apprentice saint; his sad eyes looked at the flowers like someone who has inhaled gunpowder to the point of choking.

The sun lingered, gleaming, on his shiny shaven head. But he now had only one hand and saints always have two.

When he got better, he used to smile. He didn't miss his hand. He told us in signs that he would not play with buckshot anymore. *She* had gathered up her son's little fingers and kept them in a flask of alcohol, where they swam about like happy little fishes, undoubtedly happy not to accompany my brother to the end of his life.

All of us, the fighting, the frights, were killing her precious youth.

One day, I don't even know when, we got onto the train to go to Chihuahua, Mama, little Gloria and I.

We arrived at a big hospital with lots of light and many faces bidding farewell to the sun. There you could die more comfortably: nobody weeps, there are no wakes. The brightness of the sun and the air of the mountains come right in. How nice it was! It smelled very strong, that was new for me; later I learned that that was the smell of all hospitals.

Her footsteps could be heard, light and rapid. She searched with her eyes among the group of beds she had been directed to. My thirteen-year-old brother, the eldest of all, who had gone off to join the revolution against Carranza's men, was calm and without the slightest remorse for Mama's suffering.

She, with her baby daughter in her arms, asked her son about his wound. "Would it be better in two months? Three?"

Little Gloria was about to cry. To amuse her, the wounded man in the next bed gave her a watch to play with. Play? With her little one-year-old arm she shattered it against the stone floor. Everybody laughed. The wounded man said that was what it was for, that life alone was worth being careful with. Gloriecita—her little blue eyes wild—wanted the pieces, now. She wanted to eat them.

I don't know how we returned. The train was derailed; many coaches piled on top of the engine, which remained intact, buried along with all the troops beneath what had been the track. The coaches had come apart.

What an awful thing! My eyes were accustomed to seeing death by hot lead, shattering into little pieces inside the body.

They laid out one woman in her own petticoat and tied her up like a bundle of laundry. One young man was placed carefully beside the track. You couldn't see a single mark on him, he was pale, with his eyes open. I wondered why he should stare like that; he seemed to be alive. Someone threw a handful of earth on him and blotted out his stare.

She guided us amongst all that; we, the little useless ones, her constant burden, always kept close to her skirt.

A man with a lantern told her that to get to a station where we could get some coffee and a place to sleep we would have to cross the Ortiz bridge; that the river was high, it was dangerous; that a rescue engine might come through; that he could accompany her if *She* decided to go.

The Ortiz bridge is very, very long. The Conchos River flows below, like the sea. The bridge is not meant for people on foot. The crossties are not very close together, you mustn't take a false step.

Her only reply was to place her bundles onto his shoulders. They checked the wick of the lantern. She took my little sister in her arms, grasped me by the hand: we stepped on to the bridge. On, and on, and on . . . The lantern light swung back and forth. It carried our life in its rhythm. The little strip of oil lengthened. The man was merely doing his job, but his life was his life and he was gambling it too. Our feet, our eyes, our equilibrium, our hearts, swayed over the abyss. Now I know how great was the power of her skirt and the power of her hands.

We were nearly there. We would reach the houses, drink some coffee, forget the eyes obliterated under the earth and the woman in her petticoats. How long were we walking on that bridge? A century of terror knotted itself into our hearts. The coffee slid down our bodies and bathed our feet, chiding them for their fear. *Her* voice cut into my petty, selfish meditations. "My son will arrive on Wednesday," she said in a sad tone, "the track should be repaired. Yes, he will get through all right . . ." "His mother's blessings must be reaching him," she exclaimed, looking at the long rails where we had conquered life. *She* ignored all that; she only recognized her great tenderness toward the soldier who had stayed behind in the hospital, sustained by the love *She* swathed around him.

The bridge? My fear? They didn't matter. She simply said, "You must do things quickly. That way you don't feel frightened."

One night an officer came to see her; dressed in white, with a pale face and a small black mustache. It was summertime, the moon communed with fantasy, soliciting memories and submitting to her kisses. Such was her custom: bewitched and fascinated, she would sit for hours and hours looking at the moon.

"My name is Rafael Galán," said the smiling officer, with his hat in his hand. "I have come to chat with you. May I? The moon invites one to linger here, at this doorway, where a woman drowses with a cigarette between her lips. Look at the moon. Think of your first lover. You have loved. We all love, even when it may be hopeless.

"In the revolution life makes us love a girl in every town. They have shy eyes. Sometimes we have to destroy them so that they will not destroy us; but in each woman I am loving a young girl, a mother, a child.

"This is a night of tuberoses. I have a hankering for that flower. I'll be right back," he said, nervous and smiling, and his lithe form moved like a bright shade in the darkness. She followed him with her eyes till the narrow, sad street swallowed him up in the distance.

One cigarette later, maybe two, a troop of horses thudded over the ground. Down the middle of the street came the officer surrounded by his soldiers; Rafael Galán, that officer who knew how to fire bullets and win bars for his hat and hearts for his memories.

He carried an armful of tuberoses. The street filled with perfume; he handed them down to her.

"This virginal flower was created to crown woman; tonight I want to crown you," he said sadly, taking off his hat. "We'll be leaving today. We have to attack Santa Bárbara; I would like to await our departure here, chatting with you. Will you let me? I shall smoke, I shall pay tribute to the women who, like you, are the pride of men like me, born in these northern plains."

She, who suffered with her children and on moonlit nights dreamed of love for her dead companion, listened to him enraptured. Women love, and let themselves be loved by, men who are like that.

They talked about his family, his mama who lived in Santa Bárbara, where he was to go and fight that dawn. They had orders to begin the attack at five in the morning.

Rafael Galán, tuberoses, slivers of moonlight, seated in the gray doorway with a woman, tells her his whole life and commits to her all the beauties and delicate contours of his "self," the self that was made for women and which he did not use to fire bullets.

He talked to her about his happy love affairs. A man like that always has happy love affairs. He smiled at life the way storybook gentleman captains do.

The moon, like the young lives of strong men, did not wane. It only shattered as other horsemen burst into that glorious street. Riding up to him they said, "Captain, it's time to leave."

"Yes," he said, "it is time," and shook his head. He did not want to go. "Damnation!" he said, "I have to go now, but this moon, this night . . . The moon is so lovely! I must go, but I shall return: I must return. I will not take my leave; I shall come and say good-bye one last time."

And he left, as young captains do when they go to seek death, embracing their destiny.

There was a lot of commotion. Villa's men were billeted two blocks away. There were troops everywhere. They saddled up their horses, came galloping by. Suddenly the captain stopped in front of the house. "This time it's good-bye." He had got down from his horse. He said to her, "But before I go I wish to ask a favor of you: may I embrace you?" *She* sent him off with an embrace. He kissed her hand.

He was about to remount when he quickly turned back and kissed the hem of her dress. He leaped nimbly onto his horse and rode off as only Rafael Galán could.

Three hours later the first shot of an advance party hit Rafael in the forehead. He died instantly.

Those were his last moments. He had taken his leave of what he loved best. But the white shape of the romantic officer remained there, in the gray doorway, where he took leave of life.

Captain, you were a gentleman with my mother. Tuberoses and moonlit nights belong to you.

• *She* and Her Machine •

She was singing; she was always happy when she was sewing. The noise of the machine, with its metallic chant, was the only truth of two beings in the night. *She* singing to the rhythm of the machine; the machine, a steely little girl in her hands, allowing itself to be led by her and her singing. I'd be by her side. If *She* wasn't sleepy, neither was I; if she sang, so would I.

At times I would observe her profile: a slim nose, half a mouth, the left side of her face, her hair tied back, her clear brow (I never saw her curl her hair). The profile of a strong, healthy woman went well with the profile of the machine. Her hands moved. The machine gave us hems. We needed them.

I thought, "Mama is very pretty," and would run my eyes from the tip of her nose to her mouth and to her eyes. Her eyebrows moved when she raised her voice to sing. I would follow along with her, but my voice couldn't reach that far. So I'd just go on watching her, dumb with admiration. She looked so good, she seemed so beautiful to me, that I didn't compare her with virgins or angels: I compared her only with herself.

Some of these nights, almost always, from one little gunshot, three, eight, twenty, five hundred would start up: a hailstorm of bullets. The battle would begin and in a short while turmoil would follow. When a big cannon was in action it made a noise that seemed to me as though the mouth of the sky was gaping open beside the graveyard. I shuddered with sadness; I could picture the houses crumbling. Mama would stop sewing, her face would turn watchful. "Who? Who?" her eyes would ask. She would mention names. "Can they be asleep? They must have heard the gunfire by now," she'd say to herself. "Don't let them get caught, don't let them get caught . . ."

Sometimes, when the firing was already among the houses, she would run out to save the people she loved. The machine, a clumsy doll, was abandoned; the wrinkled hems sometimes strangled the wheel, shiny like a ring of stars. The needle heartlessly chewed up the corners of those bits of fabric. What was the poor little noise of that machine compared with the shouts of the cannon? Nothing; there was no point in working it. It made me laugh to hear it alongside the cannon's song. Poor little machine that gave us hems while the cannon gave us dead bodies, lots of dead bodies! Our streets would be left strewn with those strong young bodies, scattered on the ground on top of the hems that their mamas had stitched into their shirts. What use were they? Why did they make them?

"How many pounds of flesh would they come to in total? How many eyes and thoughts? And everything about those men was dead." This was the way my precocious child's mind went. If men knew how much pity they arouse in their final pose, they would not let themselves be killed. "How many tongues? How many eyes?"

Our machine had no idea, in spite of its brilliant appearance. What could it know about this spectacle of my little girl's eyes? It could give us hems, could hum. Mama's hands would make it go again and her singing would follow the bites of the needle on the coarse dark cloth. But from this to contemplating the number of eyes, and cheeks, and fingers, was a great distance. She would sing again, the gunfire would return and I would see dead young men with rigid arms outstretched and with open mouths where flies sang. Strong men scattered there as a gift for my eyes, clutching between their fingers the hems that their mamas sewed onto the edges of their bleached clothing. But our machine would stay in its corner without knowing anything of this, and only giving us presents of patches. My dead young men were better for my lively eyes.

Parral was left alone, and when the streets were empty, the dogs cried for their masters. A savage despair gripped them. (Dogs can howl in the streets with all the strength of their lungs; they are freer than people, they must be happier.) Their dusty, tearful eyes seek people's eyes . . . They inquire, they lick their muzzles, they beg for their owners. Their desperation—unquestioning and pure—wants to see beloved faces.

A few men returned from hunting Villa. They came back routed. Then Jacinto Hernández, Petronilo's brother, became the leader of arms and the plaza was left almost empty, since there was now a mere handful of men, as they say.

These Hernández were from Río Florido. *She* knew them very well. They had been with Urbina's people, but now they were on Carranza's side. El Güero was stretched out on the Guanajuato bridge; half his head was torn off and his body crumpled up; his arms almost folded, as though he was holding on to his stomach. Jacinto fell on the left side of the bridge, going from this side to the other. Staggering—so the story went—he had taken his last steps as if he were a one-year-old child again, just beginning to walk. He clumsily almost made it to a flat piece of riverbank, but he had already left behind a large piece of his head, thrown away like something discarded because it is no longer needed and is becoming a nuisance. He crumpled up gently. He had been scattering his thoughts on the red planks where he danced his last dance and suddenly his dark body fell, creased by the bullets, spread-eagled. Jacinto stayed there embracing the sky.

They were playing cards in a house by the station. The knave and the horseman, the ace, the double draw, were interrupted. Jacinto heard some gunshots. "My boys!" he said, and ran out quickly. His second-in-command went with him. When they reached the Guanajuato bridge they heard the "who goes there?" and Jacinto replied, "Morelos Brigade." Immediately, rounds of gunfire rained on them from both sides of the bridge. The Villa boys told her that Jacinto had managed to walk from one end of the bridge to the other.

Jacinto's memory was cut short at the moment in which his simple soldier's narrow horizon included the seven of swords and the ace of cups, or perhaps the horseman of clubs—lucky, familiar, dangerous cards. The Villa soldiers drew a bull's-eye on the skewed shufflings inside poor Jacinto's head.

The dogs were still howling far off, where life disintegrated in a scream. Sometimes, in their crazy pursuit, their bodies hunched up and their eyes red from weeping, they would find their masters, their dear little gods, dumped there with their bodies full of holes and the blood pouring out, blood the dogs would lick at bit by bit, rhythmically, so gentle, so hopeful that while they wait the bodies may move suddenly and touch their little heads. They hope in vain, they lick in vain. The garbage truck arrives, or the oil tanker, or a rich coffin. Zephyr, Jupiter, and Togo howl on. Their lungs give out, slowly. Their innocent eyes also close; they will never weep again.

Sometimes dogs and children are the same. But dogs do not change. Pure desperation, real love, adoration, fill their eyes.

Jacinto Hernández, with his flashy black trousers pegged tight to his strong straight legs, stayed there with his arms wide open on the red bridge one day when they caught him on the challenge and when he staggered like a child taking its first steps.

Jiménez is a dusty little town. The streets are like hungry tripes. In the tearful night its lamps sing a sad song to the eyes as they kiss its faces. Faces that are not sad, nor resolute, but blurry like the portraits in a spiritualist seance.

This town carries in its memory the dance of the troops who made the revolution.

Facing the Plaza of the Lilacs, in a large white house with whitewashed walls and a broad patio, *She* is there and the noise of three men's voices. Sentimental song in the dark night, chinks of anemic light, a strong perfume that has no right to be where death rules and virgins won't listen to the pleas and prayers of men who foresee their end. The irresponsible lilacs, dangling from solitary trees, fulfill their mission.

Emilio, the dark, elegant officer with the ugly face, was drunk with sadness. (Romanticism was another enemy, the most dangerous. Generally those who favored the perfume of flowers and songs of love died faster than the others, since they were already poisoned.) "Valentina, Valentina, I wanted to tell you," his voice could be heard bouncing against the walls and leaving an echo that *She* repeated under her breath, swallowing the melody and smoking a cigarette, her eyes fixed in the distance, beyond the reach of my little eyes.

If I have to be killed tomorrow,
kill me once and for all . . .

The notes finished and the guitar thrummed three moments more. She turned as if hypnotized by the sound of the strings and looked at the black bulk of three men drunk on sentiments of love. Emilio got closer. This man looked washed and ironed. He greeted her sadly, the way only those who know they are in love and are not soldiers do, those born to be decorative but not to defy death.

And, nevertheless, they shot him, who knows why, one rainy night, some year or another, some day. The voice of Emilio García Hernández was never heard again. His song came true. His dark face was rotting away under the earth a month after that night in which his song failed to reach Valentina's heart.

It was in the morning. Jiménez, with its sad earth and the dusty ridges of its houses, its trees, the benches in its plaza, would offer a timid greeting so her eyes might understand without noticing the whitish dust exposed by the sun. Not like Lilac Square, silent and perfumed, a place for love, a place where life is an awkward kiss and a dream never to come true.

Jiménez, sad little place! *She* lived there and dreamed, perfuming her hands and her black locks at the lilac corner.

That morning, with little Gloria in her arms, she crossed the narrow dusty streets and went to see the Military Chief. A very bad man; he was sitting in a chair. His face was hard, angular, his eyes glassy, his nose red, with greasy open pores and a sparse, droopy mustache. When he was seated like that, behind an elegant yellow desk, he was very proper, almost good, and smiled to himself.

"I have come to take my son away," she said. "He is a child. I do not want him to be killed so young. Wait till he is a man." He laughed to himself, his mustache trembled, he rocked in his chair and sent an order for the child to be handed over to her.

They called him "Mascot," but he was Mama's son and Mama knew that flowers are worth more than diamonds and loved her son as the women of the mountains love their flowers.

There, in the Plaza of the Lilacs, half-closing her eyes, she spread out her dreams like a child who lays out her dolls before playing with them. *She* played and carried her thoughts amongst the trees, their trunks spotted with blood and their tops covered with flowers.

Lilacs of the plaza destroyed by enemy grenades, their leaves gushing with perfume, their trunks with blood, live on in the dusty town called Jiménez, perfuming Mama's tresses, which still float plaited into shadows spilling to the ground: the ground where that man fell whom Maclovio had shot with his hands tied behind him. Who was he? I only know that it happened in Lilac Square one morning when Mama was there, lost in her dreams. Eleven o'clock in the morning? Twelve? The man had rumpled black hair, reddened eyes; he was dusty all over, his eyelashes almost white. They tied him up in a corner where the dampness made shadows on the earth. His glassy eyes swiveled from side to side. He looked completely disintegrated. A few seconds later the bullets would manage to undo what he had not been able to erase from his memory. He fell there, where others had already fallen.

Mama's dreams fell, too. In Lilac Square the tree tops dance all over and the nights are still full of perfume and dreams.

When We Came to a Capital City

The long sad streets of Chihuahua greeted us with open arms. Strong, devouring arms. Indifferent eyes that kill, that constrict the spirit. The profiles of the hostile city made us shiver. The bronze statues said, "You are unreal, go back to the mountains!" And those iron monkeys stretched out their arms, "Go away!" And since they are made of metal, they stand there still, pointing at the mountain.

An ugly house in a wide street, a small piece of sky in the patio. A number that says 25 and drafts of wind that lash the body and enter right into the corners. Outside, people's faces are sad, with dull eyes, tight mouths. Bitter city, creeping into the nightmares of those who have been unlucky enough to land there. It steals all impetus, shrinks the spirit, crushes one's brain power. The best is found outside, in the mountains, where the people are serene as big children, with transparent dreams: simple, good, free, beautiful, strong and agile like the mountain deer that cross the desert and climb the peaks, balancing their bodies in the crannies. Handsome race of the plains of Chihuahua: I like them, I admire them as I do the Tarahumaras, ancient Indians, peaceful, sensitive, artistic, exponents of a noble life, resigned by nature albeit without the civilization of the white man. They carry their compliance to staying ignorant of money and only recognize people's smiles.

It is the month of December. Our tribe in the warmth of the coals. Since its world lies there, the ugly faces and streets don't matter. In her arms *She* holds a little blond angel with blue eyes and strong shoulders, a true representative of a race of warrior antecedents that today, converted into a sentimental tribe, lives in a street called 25.

My brothers were going to school, twisted their voices when they spoke, made rude jokes with new-learned words, scribbled, stuck out their tongues as they sharpened their pencils and made a lot of noise with their clear, liquid infantile voices. "Oh! Nuisances!" (I said out loud). That was when I started to distance myself from their friendship; I was unsure of their disobedience, they had greatly betrayed me. My solitude was absolute. The crags, the hills and the fields were my refuge. I didn't want school. Why should I have to be with nagging people? You only go there to suffer, to learn class distinctions, to put up with some teacher's ailment: a hysterical or a diabetic miss or a sir with liver problems or some disease of the kidneys or the mouth. No, no, no. Are these sick beings the ones who should form children's spirit? No, no. But in fact, I really did not know why I didn't like school. I fought against going and *She* did not force me. My brothers wanted school, books, First Communion, and they were given them. Undoubtedly they picked up all their lies from being there, at school, mixed in with boys who had the obsessions of little old men.

I saw many girls who fulfilled their month for Mary. They wore veils on their heads, flowers and a rosary in their hands, all the trappings of church going, and it never occurred to me to do the same. I was also afraid of being taken to church. Confession? First Communion? "No, no, no," I said, wriggling my shoulders and gritting my teeth. *She* did not force me now, either.

My temperament needed freedom, and since *She* knew that, she left me alone. One day Doña Isabel, an aunt of mine, taught me how to read. I wanted to do it and it wasn't hard. I learned how to write. I knew everything. My aunt was a very serious lady, with pretty white teeth. Everything I learned then, my aunt taught me.

She was happy to see her children's progress and was happy too when I proffered her my ruddy freckled face and showed off my prowess on horseback. It was so easy to learn everything without sitting for hours and hours with a bent back on a hard bench! Sometimes, as she sensed the hoofbeats of a horse galloping past *She* would say: "That's my wild tomboy daughter. She is a real Comanche. If my father could see her, he would be proud of her."

The other children would read, do their sums, pile up on top of each other near the light like real butterflies. I wasn't one of them. To myself I thought very simple thoughts. I always preferred strong feet and sturdy legs. Why should infant kidneys be sacrificed on sinister school benches?

It is true that I prefer a character and a body formed within a pure and cake-free life. A strong healthy child who can't read is better than a sickly, clever one. It is so easy to rear a healthy child and so difficult to straighten a twisted spine!

The little angel was growing bigger. Mama watched as those nine-month-old legs took their first steps. His feet grew strong, could run and scuff the tips of his sandals. He could shout, pronounce words. He would open his arms and fall laughing into her lap.

With his still unformed voice he asked for a gun, a horse, a bicycle, and said "Kill. . . my gu. . . man . . . tigger. . . Go street bikey. My horsie . . . Oops my Mama Lala. Up Uncle Moya come bogeyman. . . my Mama. Hand hurts, silly. . . Siste take." His half words filled every corner of the house. Sadness, drought, worries, everything faded away under his chatter. He ran everywhere, scribbled on bits of paper. He rode his bicycle, wore his pistol, and always the sound of his voice: a constant dialogue carried all over the house, lighting up our faces as we watched over his little movements. One day, swinging on a door panel, he told his Mama Lala that he was going away . . . "Go . . . lon way my Lala, go." Three more days and he'd gone.

She went mad. . . She was dying on us. . . Her eyes dried up. . . She could not live.

At night she would go to the cemetery. She would stay there. At six in the morning she would return disconsolate, sad, tearful. She would not eat, would not sleep, begged for death.

The Virgin of Solitude, a lady in a long dress covered with a solemn cloak, her hands aristocratically joined to hold the corner of a lace handkerchief and around her head a radiance that made her face more sorrowful, ended up in the middle of the street with her grieving face in pieces. The Lady of Solitude with her infinite power could not halt the pneumonia that split the strong shoulders of the child. The watch was shattered against the floor. It had stopped at the exact moment of departure.

The little blond angel was no more. *She* would not believe it. But, his little voice? And his little footsteps that came and went with the bits of words? It was true. He was not there. But *She* did not believe it and would go to the grave on dark nights and keep vigil there over the son who had carried off her happiness.

Months went by. She saw that he would not come back in spite of her offering our lives—she being their mistress—in piles in exchange for the life of the child which had wiped out the happiness from our home; she asked to die.

Her hands, in a decisive gesture, rejected life.

September came. Fireworks, bright colors, paper hats and chains, squibs, alcohol, shouts. . .

As always, *She* hastened her step to get to where she was needed most. Her gaze carried her far, far away. . .

They did not cover her with flowers. They crossed her hands, they lit up her face with candles.

Her smile like a timid child, the way her body lay, everything about her seemed to beg pardon from life.

She went away. . .

Nothing that I write to you contains shadows: *You* want us to go happily on, stepping in rhythm to the place where *You* wait.

Today is the day, it is six in the afternoon; he called to you and *You* went to a heaven that both of you knew about.

You wanted to go, that is clear. How strange it seems, but how obvious! With such a great desire to leave, Mother, and watching life lengthen one second at a time, you shut off your eyes, so that you would not feel it.

You bequeathed us your laughter, you bequeathed us your joy; that is why when we close our eyes today we can see you and laugh with you as we did in those moments of sadness when you taught us how.

I am sending this to you on the wind, to the far-off sky where you live and watch us wait for your hands to unfold one day so that we may worship you.

Here, Mama:

It is the beginning of an autumn month; *You* are at the foot of the mountains waiting to return to the place of your star. To the beautiful place you showed us.

Following your hand, we are still here, watching you. The threads of veins between your hands are woven through you. True, clear smiles are yours. And in the same way, everything that flowers for us—is yours. Life gave you our pain and took all you had away from you, but now we are trying to accomplish what you would have wished. And we came back constantly to look for you. The light of comprehension is slow, and grief wells up, grief formed from presentiment.

A far-off graveyard, a gray and blue mountain, a flowerless grave. *You* wait there for your children's hands to come and stir the earth where your eyes rested forever. The earth pressing on your dear bones blooms, and *You* come toward us.

You arrive and our hope is sustained in your image. We want you here, come back. Mama:

If *You* came back, your last satin slippers, your stockings, the two little spoons that your lips used, your pack of cards, the breadcrumbs, you would find everything you left just the same; our hearts have in no way changed toward you.

A heart made by your companion, and which adorned your neck, is waiting here for your hands to come and touch it.

The white box for your brooches, with your tuberoses, your dahlias, your hairclips, and containing the last smiles of your simple brown eyes, the eyes that now, far away, must be ashes, also wait for you.

I remember your hands, those brave hands that were born to give to us and to guide us; your woman's hands, your companions, your best friends. We bend in prayer:

They raised us and showed us the way. The best way, the one that goes straight, through the snow, the mountains, the quarries, the mud, the blue rivers, the filthy huts and the graveyards.

They gave us life. They plaited our hair, washed our faces, and dried our eyes.

They made the sign of the cross on our foreheads, and made wheat blossom into clusters of tortillas. The movement of your hands was adorable, gentle; they looked like flowers carried in the streams that run down the mountains. Your hands were like doves, settling into place with burgeoning wings. I swear by the gentle hair on your adorable head. By the clouds that dance under the motion of the sun. By the pulsing of my heart and all the profiles and sacred images that my people keep.

So white, so soft, so perfect.

Mama, turn your face, look at us, smile, stretch out your hands. . .

She was as graceful as the flowers of the mountain. . .
Her eyes, golden spikes;
Her hands, tight grains of wheat. . .
Her tears. . .
Her skirt dances, dances in the wind. . .
She is there on the horizon, she does not turn her face.

It is sunset in the north. . . A red evening, extended into the veins of her hands, the hands that tore her blouse to find her god. . .

CPSIA information can be obtained
at www.ICGtesting.com
Printed in the USA
LVHW090112150420
653513LV00001B/105

9 780292 711112